# This is Lagos
# and other stories

# ABOUT THE AUTHOR

Flora Nwapa is Nigeria's first woman novelist, author of the highly praised *Efuru, Idu, Women are Different, Never Again, Wives at War* and *One is Enough*.

FLORA NWAPA

# THIS IS LAGOS
## AND OTHER STORIES

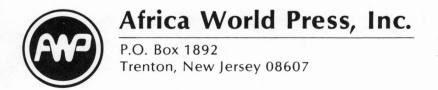

**Africa World Press, Inc.**

P.O. Box 1892
Trenton, New Jersey 08607

Africa World Press, Inc.
P.O. Box 1892
Trenton, New Jersey 08607


First published in Nigeria by TANA PRESS, 1971


© Copyright Flora Nwapa 1971, 1992


First Africa World Press edition 1992

Cover design and illustration: Ife Designs

ISBN:  0-86543-320-8 Cloth
       0-86543-321-6 Paper

Editorial Adviser
# CHINUA ACHEBE

*For Clara & A.Y.*

# CONTENTS

Page

# The Traveller

There was a knock at the door and Bisi went to open it.

'Good afternoon, please come right in.'

'You remember me, don't you?' the stranger asked.

'I remember the face, but not the name,' Bisi lied.

'We were together at College.'

'Of course it was at College. Please sit down, and where are you now?' Bisi asked. It was obvious that she still could not place the man.

'I am in Lagos and have come to do some business here. I thought I should come and say hello to you. You were in Edinburgh last year, weren't you? I saw you for a brief time while in the company of Obi and his sisters.'

'You are right,' Bisi said remembering her holidays in Edinburgh, but she still could not place the man.

'How are you enjoying teaching?'

'I love it. I did not know I would enjoy it so much.'

'I am glad to hear this. Many people get bored with it in no time, and look around for something more exciting.'

'You are right. It all depends on the individual. Where do you work in Lagos?' Bisi asked.

'I work with a firm of experts. We give our expert advice to the public on buildings and so on.'

'And you are enjoying it, aren't you?'

'It is exciting. I do a lot of touring. In December, I was in the Cameroons. After this trip, I shall come more frequently to the East.'

'And how long are you staying here?' she asked.

'I leave for Ogoja tomorrow, Onitsha next tomorrow, and

1

on Saturday, I go to Port Harcourt.'

'That's grand. I like touring,' Bisi said, getting up. 'I am sorry Mr. . . .'

'Mr. Musa,' the stranger said promptly.

'Mr. Musa, I must go to my lesson now. The children are waiting for me.'

'And I must be going too. Thank you very much. Are you free this evening?'

'Sorry, I am not free.'

'You are free tomorrow afternoon then?'

'Yes, tomorrow afternoon, I am free, but you are going to Ogoja.'

'I shall be back before lunch time. Can you come to lunch with me at the hotel?'

'That is very kind of you. But it is a shame that you should come all the way from Lagos and invite me to lunch. I should invite you to a meal in my house.'

'Oh, that does not matter at all. Anywhere I go, I could ask as many people to meals as I want. It costs me nothing. The pleasure is mine. When do I come for you?'

'One thirty.'

'I shall be here at one thirty, then. See you.'

'Bye bye.'

'My God, isn't he talkative?' Bisi said as soon as Mr. Musa's driver drove away. She wondered whether he was actually at College with her, and blamed herself for accepting the lunch appointment.

However, at one thirty the next day, Mr. Musa was in Bisi's house, Bisi came out and they drove to the hotel.

'How was your trip to Ogoja?'

'Fine. I am making headway, and I am very happy.'

A taxi, hooted and overtook Mr. Musa at a very dangerous corner, and stopped not quite thirty yards in front.

'These taxi drivers should not be given licences,' Mr. Musa said.

'They know what to do. It is just sheer irresponsibility and

2

lack of patience. What makes me mad is when they abuse you when they are wrong,' Bisi said.

'I guess you just go your way when they abuse you,' Mr. Musa said laughing.

'Of course I don't. I abuse them and talk to them in the language they understand. I am not a lady when it comes to that.'

Mr. Musa laughed. 'That's what I do too.'

'Shall we have some drinks?' Musa asked as they arrived at the hotel. 'What would you like to drink?'

'Babycham,' she replied.

'That's good. I like Babycham myself, but I will have a small Star.'

'Good afternoon, doc,' Bisi greeted a man who came in.

'Hello Bisi, how are you?'

'Very well, thank you. How is the battle?'

'Still raging. Do you know the latest?'

'No, what are you up to now?'

'Well, we were there as usual. We sat down at our seats. Patients came, we took a full report, wrote everything down in long hand, took the patient in and examined him fully, and called in the next patient. In this way, by twelve o'clock no doctor saw more than three patients.'

'Hello, doc.'

'How are you, Musa, when did you come?'

'A couple of days ago.'

'Nice to see you.'

'Yes doc, you have a case,' Bisi said.

'You mean private practice for doctors?' Mr. Musa asked.

'Yes, P.P. for doctors. They have a case, haven't they?' Bisi said.

'Yes, but unscrupulous doctors could easily abuse it.'

'Excuse me,' the doctor said and left.

They selected a table for two.

'Are you going to have pounded yam?'

'No, when I come here, I want to eat something different. And besides I am slimming.'

3

'Women are always slimming. Oh that's a good high life music. Do you like it?'

'I like it, but I don't like listening to high life music,' she replied.

'Why?' he asked.

'I like to dance to high life music.'

'That's a good one,' he said.

When they finished eating, they went to his room. He tuned his radio, and waltz music was playing, very softly.

'Let's dance, shall we?'

'Dance?' she asked in suprise. 'I have just eaten. I can't do any dancing now.' He laughed and did not insist.

'By the way, I hear Dora Okeke is here. Can we see her tonight?'

'Oh yes, what time?'

'About nine o'clock.'

'That's late, make it eight.'

'You see, someone is taking me out at seven, and I guess I will be free at nine.'

'All right, nine then. I must go now. I haven't had siesta.'

'There are two beds.'

'No, thank you,' she said.

He came near her and put his hands round her neck. There was no response. He took her hands in his and squeezed them. The effect was the same.

'What is the matter?' he asked

'With what?' she replied. He left her.

'I shall take you back now.'

'That is thoughtful of you.'

He drove her home.

Mr. Musa arrived at nine thirty full of apologies.

'Lets go now,' Bisi said and called her maid who locked the door. 'Helen,' Bisi called, 'please bring my wallet. I have no money on me and I may buy some petrol.'

'Oh don't bother. It is all right,' Mr. Musa said.

'No. Helen, please bring my wallet quickly. It is in the cupboard.'

4

'I said don't bother.'

'I can't find it,' Helen said.

'I said let's go.'

They arrived at a petrol station and Mr. Musa filled the tank for her, and got a receipt. When they arrived at Dora's school, she was not in.

'What do we do now? It is too early to go to bed,' Musa said.

'It is ten fifteen, you know I can't go to bed before midnight.'

'All right. Let's visit a friend of mine.'

'Who is he?'

'It is a she. You know Nwakama at College?'

'Okechukwu Nwakama?'

'Yes, Okechukwu. He is my friend's fiancee.'

In five minutes they were in Sophia's house. They were introduced.

'And when is the lucky man coming home?'

'Next year,' Sophia replied. 'Can I offer you beer?'

'Yes, provided you share it with me.'

'We don't drink beer here. We are bush.'

'I know you are not bush. You will share it with me.'

'All right. We will share it,' Bisi said.

Beer was brought and the two girls had half a glass each which they did not enjoy. When they finished, they got up to go. Bisi drove to her house, and as she said good night to Musa, he drew her to him.

'Don't be in a hurry. Kiss me good night.'

Bisi pushed him away. He wanted to come near again, but thought better of it and said, 'I shall see you tomorrow at eight. We shall collect Sophia and have supper or drinks somewhere. Good night.'

'Good night,' Bisi said and shut the door.

The next evening at eight, Bisi collected Sophia. Mr. Musa was picked from his hotel and they went out to have drinks. All the places they went to were interesting, and at about eleven o'clock they decided to go home.

'Take Sophia home first,' Musa suggested.

'Yes take me home first,' Sophia echoed.

Bisi laughed and reversed the car. Sophia was seen safely home. She then drove Mr. Musa to his hotel.

'Good night,' she said not turning off the engine.

'No, you must come in.'

'No, it is late, and I must rise early tomorrow morning.'

'I know. Come in for a few minutes.'

'No,' she said and shook her head vigorously.

'This is most unfair, Bisi. Please come in. You can go any time you want to go. I won't stop you.'

'No.'

He locked his side of the car, came to her side and took her by the hand. She allowed her hand to be taken, but she remained doggedly on her seat.

'All right. If you don't want to go in, let's go for a walk.'

'For a walk, at this time of the night, not me.'

'What do you want me to do now?' Musa asked in despair.

'Go to bed and let me go home.'

'You have refused to come in?'

'Yes, I have refused to come in.'

'What is your reason?'

'Reason, you don't do things always with reason.' Musa went into the room and came back.

'What about this cocktail party tomorrow night?' he asked.

'I am not invited.'

'Oh, don't be impossible. You said yesterday you will go with me.'

'So I said. Can't I change my mind?'

'This is hopeless. We shall go, Bisi.'

'I don't want to gate-crash,' Bisi said laughing.

'The guest of honour and I were classmates. I saw him only yesterday and I assured him I would be there. Please Bisi, be reasonable.' He opened the door of the car and went in. 'Drive me to anywhere,' he said. Bisi laughed and said nothing.

6

'Please, Bisi please.'

'All right, I shall go with you. When is the party?'

'Come at four or five.'

'For the cocktail party?' she asked in surprise.

'Can't you come at that time?' he asked.

'I shall come at seven o'clock. Good night.'

'Look, Bisi, this is most unfair. Please just go into that room, then come out. I shall be here, I promise.'

She shook her head vigorously. He took a deep breath, and sighed. 'Good night then. I shall see you tomorrow.'

At seven o'clock, Bisi was in Mr. Musa's hotel.

'Can I drive you tonight?'

'Oh, never mind. When you go back to Lagos, tell your friends you had a woman chauffeur in Enugu.'

'You are going to eat goat meat,' Bisi said to Mr. Musa.

'Goat meat at a cocktail party?'

'Of course, when there is no goat meat, the guests demand it by right. It must be brought.'

It was not a bad cocktail. But it was the same pattern. One heard the usual questions asked at parties. 'How is the car behaving?' Conversations on promotions. Nothing on the international or national level whatever. They called on one or two people, filled Bisi's tank again and drove to the hotel. When they arrived there, Mr. Musa came out and banged his side of the door. Bisi remained as yesterday, in her seat.

'Oh please, let's not do this all over again tonight.'

She said nothing. She remained doggedly again on her seat and did not even switch off the engine.

'Come, Bisi, let's go in. It is only eleven thirty. When you want to go home, I shall not keep you.'

'I am not coming out. What am I coming out for?'

'When you come out, you will know.'

She laughed.

'After all, we are adults and responsible. Why are you behaving so childishly? Why are you doing this to me?' He opened the car, took her handbag and placed it on the bonnet of the car.

7

'When you want to go, go and take your handbag,' he said laughing.

'You are clever, aren't you?' Bisi said.

Mr. Musa forced his way into the driver's seat. 'Oh no, don't do that. You are hurting me. You know this seat is only meant for one person.'

'The way you talk, Bisi, well, I must confess one thing.'

'Go ahead.'

'I am not in love, but I feel as if I am.'

'And how many times do you feel like that in a week?' she asked laughing. She was not disappointed.

He did not say a word. That was not what he expected. For some time, they did not talk.

'Come on, let's go in, Bisi.' Bisi shook her head.

'Why do you stay there shaking your head at everything I say?'

She did not of course say a word.

'Look, as I said before,' Mr. Musa began again, 'I am not in love, but . . .'

'I am not in love either, or do you think I should be?' Bisi said firmly. The cheek of him to repeat it.

There was a long silence.

'Will I see you tomorrow?' Mr. Musa asked.

'When does your plane leave?' Bisi asked.

'About twelve twenty.'

'I shall come at eleven to drive you to the airport.'

'Can't you come earlier than that?'

'No, I can't.'

He came closer and kissed her. But she did not return the kiss. She switched on the engine, was about to drive off when he said urgently, 'Wait.' He opened the car and went in. Bisi looked at him in surprise. 'Won't you let me go. It is one a.m.'

'You don't seem to believe me. What I have been doing has been the accumulation of my feelings for you for a long time, even at College.'

'Really?'

8

'You don't seem to believe me, Bisi.'

'Does it really matter whether I believe you or not. I thought that what mattered was whether you yourself believe what you have just said.'

She started the car again. Mr. Musa came out willingly and she drove off.

Bisi told her friend Sophia everything the next morning. Both girls went to see Mr. Musa. He was ready to go to the airport.

'You are lucky to have two beautiful women to see you off,' Sophia said.

'Well, maybe I may not even have one after all. Your friend is unkind,' he said.

They did not wait long before the plane took off. And as Bisi and Sophia were driving back home, Bisi began to laugh.

'Why are you laughing?'

'Musa, what kind of man is he? And what kind of woman does he think I am?'

# This is Lagos

'They say Lagos men do not just chase women, they snatch them,' Soha's mother told her on the eve of her departure to Lagos. 'So my daughter be careful. My sister will take care of you. You should help her with her housework and her children, just as you have been doing here.'

Soha was fond of her aunt. She called her Mama Eze. Eze was her aunt's first son. And Mama Eze called Soha my sister's daughter. She too was fond of Soha whom she looked after when she was a little girl.

Soha was a sweet girl. She was just twenty when she came to Lagos. She was not beautiful in the real sense of the word. But she was very pretty and charming. She was full of life. She pretended that she knew her mind, and showed a confidence rare in a girl who had all her education in a village.

Her aunt and her family lived in Shomolu in the outskirts of Lagos. There was a primary school nearby, and it was in the school that her uncle by marriage got her a teaching job. Soha did not like teaching, but there was no other job, and so, like so many teachers, the job was just a stepping stone.

In the morning before she went to school, Soha saw that her aunt's children, five in all, were well prepared for school. She would see that they had their baths, wore their uniforms, and looked neat and tidy. Then she prepared their breakfast, and before seven each morning, the children were ready to go to school.

Everybody in the 'yard' thought how dutiful Soha was. Her aunt's husband who was a quiet man praised Soha, and told his wife that she was a good girl. Her aunt was proud of her. Since she came to stay with them, her aunt had had time for relaxation, she did less housework, and paid more attention to her trade, which was selling bread.

For some time, everything went well with them. But Mama Eze did not like the way Soha refused to go on holiday when the school closed at the end of the first term. She was surprised when Soha told her that she did not want to go home to see her mother, despite the fact that her mother had been ill, and was recovering.

'Why don't you want to go home, my sister's daughter?'

'Who will look after the children if I go home?' she asked.

Mama Eze did not like the tone of Soha's voice. 'Who had been looking after the children before you came, my sister's daughter? Your mother wants you to come home. You know how fond she is of you. I don't want her to think that I prevented you from coming home.'

'She won't think so. I shall go during the Christmas holiday. This is a short holiday, only three weeks. And the roads. Remember what Lagos-Onitsha road is like.' But she did not go home during the Christmas holiday either.

It was that argument that sort of did the trick. Mama Eze remembered the accident she witnessed not long ago. She was returning from the market, a huge load on her head, when, just in a flash it happened. It was a huge tipper-lorry and a Volkswagen car. She saw blood, and bodies, and the wreck of the Volkswagen. She covered her face with her hands. When she opened them, she looked the other way, and what did she see, a human tongue on the ground.

When she returned home, she told her husband. She swore that from thenceforth she would travel home by train.

She did not suggest going home by train to her niece. Soha had long rejected that idea. She did not see the sanity of it all. Why should a man in Lagos, wishing to go to Port Harcourt decide to go up to Kaduna in the North first, then down south to Port Harcourt, and to take three days and three nights doing the journey he would do in a few hours if he

11

were travelling by road.

One Saturday, during the holiday a brand new car stopped in front of the big 'yard.' The children in the 'yard' including Mama Eze's children trooped out to have a closer look. A young man stepped out of the car and asked one of the children whether Soha lived there. 'Yes, sister Soha lives here. Let me go and call her for you,' Eze said, and ran into the house.

Soha was powdering her face when Eze pushed open the door and announced, 'Sister Soha, a man is asking for you. He came in a car, a brand new car. I have not seen that car before. Come and see him. He wants you.' Eze held her hand and began dragging her to the sitting room. 'No Eze, ask him to sit down in the sitting room and wait for me,' Soha said quietly to Eze. Eze dropped her hand and ran outside again. 'She is coming. She says I should ask you to sit down in the sitting room and wait for her,' he said to the man. The man followed him to the sitting room.

The children stood admiring the car. 'It is a Volkswagen,' one said. 'How can that be a Volkswagen? It is a Peugeot,' another said. 'Can't you people see? It is a Rekord,' yet another child said. They were coming close now. Some were touching the body of the car and leaving their dirty fingerprints on it when Eze came out again and drove them out. 'Let me see who says he is strong, dare come near this car.' He planted himself in front of the car, looking bigger than he really was.

'Does the car belong to Eze's father?' a child asked.

'No. It belongs to sister Soha's friend,' one of Eze's brothers replied without hesitation.

'I thought it belonged to your father,' the same child said again.

'Keep quiet. Can't my father buy a car?' Eze shouted standing menacingly in front of the child.

Soha was still in front of the mirror admiring herself. She was not in a hurry at all. Her mother had told her that she

12

should never show a man that she was anxious about him. She should rather keep him waiting as long as she wished. She was wearing one of the dresses she sewed for herself when she was at home. She suddenly thought of changing it. But she changed her mind, and instead came out. She was looking very shy as she took the outstretched hand of the man who had come to visit her.

'Are you ready?'

'For . . .'

'We are going to Kingsway Stores.'

'Kingsway Stores?'

'Of course. But we discussed it last night, and you asked me to come at nine thirty,' the man said looking at his watch.

'I am sorry. But I can't go again.'

'You can't go?'

'No.'

'Why?'

'Can't I change my mind?'

'Of course you can,' the man said quietly a little surprised.

'I am going then.'

'Already?'

'Yes.'

'Don't you work on Saturdays?'

'No.'

'Go well then,' Soha said

'When am I seeing you again?'

'I don't know. I have no car.'

'Let's go to the cinema tonight.'

'No, my mother will kill me.'

'Your aunt.'

'Yes. She is my mother. You said you will buy something for me today.'

'Let's go to the Kingsway Stores then. I don't know how to buy things for women.'

'Don't you buy things for your wife?'

'I told you, I have no wife.' Soha laughed long and loud. The man watched her.

'Who are you deceiving? Please go to your wife and don't bother me. Lagos men, I know Lagos men.'

'How many of them do you know?' She did not answer. She rather rolled her eyes and shifted in the chair in which she sat.

'I am going,' he said standing up.

'Don't go now,' she said. They heard the horn of a car.

'That's my car,' he said.

'So?'

'The children are playing with the horn.'

'So?'

'You are exasperating! I like you all the same. Let's go to this shopping, Soha. What is wrong with you? You are so stubborn.'

'No, I won't go. I shall go next Saturday. I did not tell Mama Eze.'

'You said you would.'

'So I said.'

He got up. It did not seem to him that there would be an end to this conversation.

'You are going?'

'I am going.'

'Wait, I'll come with you.' He breathed in and breathed out again.

'Go and change then.'

'Change. Don't you like my dress?'

'I like it, but change into a better dress.'

'I have no other dress. I might as well stay. You are ashamed of me.'

'You have started again.'

'I won't go again. How dare you say that my dress is not respectable. Well, maybe you will buy dresses for me before I go out with you.' He put his hand in his back pocket and brought out his wallet. He pressed a five pound note into her hand. She smiled and they went out.

'Eze, you have been watching his car?' Soha said.

Eze nodded. He dipped into his pocket and gave Eze a

14

shilling. Eze jumped with joy.

'We watched with him,' the other children chorused.

'Yes. They watched with him,' Soha said. He brought out another shilling and gave to them. Then he drove away.

Mama Eze did not know about the young man who visited Soha. Soha warned the children not to tell their parents. But it was obvious to her that Soha had secrets. It was easy for a mother of five children who had watched so many girls growing up in the 'yard' to know when they were involved in men. At first, she thought of asking Soha, but she thought better of it until one day when Soha told her she was going to the shops and did not come back until late in the evening. She called her in.

'Where did you go, my sister's daughter?'

'I told you I went to the shops.'

'Many people went to the shops from this "yard", but they returned long before you.'

'Well, we did not go to the same shops,' Soha said. Mama Eze did not like the way Soha talked to her. She smiled. 'Soha,' she called her. That was the first time Mama Eze called her by her name. 'Soha,' she called again. 'This is Lagos. Lagos is different from home. Lagos is big. You must be careful here. You are a mere child. Lagos men are too deep for you. Don't think you are clever. You are not. You can never be cleverer than a Lagos man. I am older than you are, so take my advice.'

Soha said nothing. She did not give a thought to what her aunt told her. But that night, Mama Eze did not sleep well. She told her husband. 'You worry yourself unnecessarily. Didn't she tell you before she went to the shops?'

'She did.'

'Well then?'

'Well then,' Mama Eze echoed mockingly. 'Well then. Go on speaking English, "well then". When something happens to Soha now, you will stay there. This is the time you should do something.'

'Why are you talking like that, Mama Eze? What has the

15

girl done? She is such a nice girl. She doesn't go out. She has been helping you with your housework. You yourself say so.'

Mama Eze said nothing to him any more. One evening when Soha returned from school, she asked her aunt if she would allow her to go to the cinema. Her aunt clapped her hands in excitement, and rushed out of the room. 'Mama Bisi, come out and hear what Soha is saying.'

Mama Bisi who was her neighbour came out. 'What did she say?' she asked clasping her chest. She was afraid.

'Soha, my sister's daughter, wants to go to the cinema.' Mama Bisi hissed. 'Is that all? You are excited because she has told you today. What about the other nights she has been going?'

'Other nights? Other nights?'

'Go and sit down *Ojari*. You don't know what you are saying. Soha, your sister's daughter, has been going out with different men for a long time now. You don't even see the dresses she wears, and the shoes. Do they look like the dresses a girl like her would wear?'

Mama Eze said nothing. Soha said nothing. 'When Papa Eze returns, ask him whether you can go to the cinema,' Mama Eze finally said after looking at her niece for a long time.

It wasn't long after this that Soha came to her aunt and told her that she wanted to move to a hostel.

'To a hostel, my sister's daughter. Who will pay for you?'

'I receive a salary.'

'I see. I know you receive a salary. Those of us who have never received salaries in our lives know about salaries. But why now? Why do you want to leave us now? Don't you like my home any more? Is it too small for you? Or too humble? Are you ashamed of entertaining your friends here?'

'I want to start reading again. That's why I want to move to a hostel. It will be more convenient for me there.'

'That is true. When you sing well, the dancer dances well. I understand my sister's daughter. I have to tell my husband and my sister. Your mother said you should stay with me. It

16

is only reasonable that I tell her that you are leaving me to go to a hostel. What hostel is that by the way?'

'The one at Ajagba Street.'

'I see.'

When Soha went to school, Mama Eze went over to Mama Bisi and told her what Soha said. 'I have told you,' Mama Bisi said. 'Soha is not a better girl. Do you know the kind of girls who live in that hostel at Ajagba Street? Rotten girls who will never marry. No man will bring them into his home and call them wives. You know that my sister who is at Abeokuta whom I went to see last week?'

'Yes, I know her. Iyabo.'

'That's right. Iyabo. One of her friends who stayed in that hostel, nearly took Iyabo there. I stopped it. As soon as I heard it, I went to her mother at Abeokuta and told her. She came down, and both of us went to her. After talking to her, she changed her mind. So that's the place Soha wants to go and live. I no tell you, they say to go Lagos no hard, na return. Soha will be lost if she goes there.'

Mama Eze returned home one evening from the market and was told that Soha had not been home from school. She put down her basket of unsold bread and sat down. 'Didn't she tell you where she went?' she asked Eze. Eze shook his head. 'And where is your father?' Mama Eze asked Eze.

'He has gone out.'

'Where has he gone?'

'I don't know.'

'You don't know. Every question, you don't know. Do you think you are still a child? Let me have some water quickly.' Eze brought the water. Then Eze's father returned.

'They say Soha has not returned home,' Mama Eze said to her husband.

'So Eze told me.'

'And you went out, because Soha is not your sister. If Soha were your sister you would have been hysterical.'

Then Mama Bisi came in, and sat down. She had heard of course.

17

'Eze, why not tell them the truth?' Mama Bisi said. Eze said nothing.

'Eze, so you know where Soha went?' Mama Eze asked. 'I don't know,' Eze protested vehemently.

'You helped Soha with her box. I saw you,' Mama Bisi accused.

She did not see Eze do this, but what she said was true. Mama Eze and her husband were confused.

'Mama Bisi, please, tell me what you know.'

'Ask your son there. He know everything. He knows where Soha went.'

'I don't know. You are lying, Mama Bisi.' Mama Eze got up and slapped Eze's face. 'How dare you, how dare you say that Mama Bisi is lying, you, you good-for-nothing child.'

'Ewo, Mama Eze, that will do. If you slap the boy again, you'll have it hot.'

'*Jo* don't quarrel,' Mama Bisi begged. She went over to Papa Eze. 'Please don't. But Eze, you are a bad child. Why are you hiding evil? A child like you behaving in this way.'

Eze knew a lot. He helped Soha pack her things, and it was the gentleman with the car who took Soha away. Soha told him not to breathe a word to anybody. She also told him that she and her husband would come in the night to see his parents.

As they were wondering what to do, Eze slipped out. He was the only one who heard the sound of the car. He had grown to like Soha's friend since the day he watched his car for him. And he had also had many rides in his car as well, for anywhere Soha's friend saw Eze, he stopped to give him a lift, and he had enjoyed this very much.

Soha and the gentleman stepped out of the car, Soha leading the way. Mama Eze, Mama Bisi and Papa Eze stared at them. Soha and her friend stood. They stared at them.

'Can we sit down?' Soha asked as she sat down. The gentleman stood.

'Sit down,' Papa Eze said. He sat down.

None found words. Soha's gentleman was completely lost.

18

'Is Soha living with you?' Papa Eze asked after a long time.
'Yes,' he said.
'In fact we were married a month ago,' Soha said.
'No,' Mama Eze shouted. 'You, you married to my sister's daughter. Impossible. You are going to be "un-married". Do you hear? Mama Bisi, is that what they do here?'
'This is Lagos. Anything can happen here,' Mama Bisi said. Then she turned to the gentleman and spoke in Yoruba to him. It was only Papa Eze who did not understand.
'It is true, Papa Eze. They are married. What is this country turning into? Soha, you, you who left home only yesterday to come to Lagos, you are married, married to a Lagos man, without telling anybody. It is a slight and nothing else. What do I know? I didn't go to school. If I had gone to school, you wouldn't have treated me in this way.'
'So you pregnated her,' Mama Bisi said to Soha's husband in Yoruba. He did not immediately reply. Soha's heart missed a beat. 'So it is showing already,' she said to herself. Mama Bisi smiled bitterly. 'You children. You think you can deceive us. I have seven children.'
'What is your name?' Mama Bisi asked Soha's husband in Yoruba.
'Ibikunle,' he replied.
'Ibikunle, we don't marry like this in the place where we come from . . .' Mama Eze did not finish.
'Even in the place where he comes from *kpa kpa*,' Mama Bisi interrupted. 'It is Lagos. When they come to Lagos they forget their home background. Imagine coming here to say they are married. Where in the world do they do this sort of thing?'
'You hear, Mr. Ibikunle, we don't marry like that in my home,' Mama Eze said. 'Home people will not regard you as married. This is unheard of. And you tell me this is what the white people do. So when white people wish to marry, they don't seek the consent of their parents, they don't even inform them. My sister's daughter,' she turned to Soha, 'you have not done well. You have rewarded me with evil. Why

19

did you not take me into confidence? Am I not married? Is marriage a sin? Will I prevent you from marrying? Isn't it the prayer of every woman?'

'It is enough Mama Eze,' Mama Bisi said. 'And besides . . .'

'You women talk too much. Mr. Ibikunle has acted like a gentleman. What if he had run away after pregnating Soha. What would you do?'

'Hear what my husband is saying. I don't blame you. What am I saying? Aren't you a man. Aren't all men the same? Mr. Ibikunle, take your wife to your house, and get ready to go home to see your father and mother-in-law. I'll help you with the preparations.'

Husband and wife went home. Mama Eze went home and told Soha's parents what had happened. A whole year passed. Mr. Ibikunle did not have the courage, or was it the money to travel to Soha's home to present himself to Soha's parents as their son-in-law?

# Jide's Story

We met in England. She was from a village near my home. I
met her at a dance. I had heard she was in London, but
hadn't seen her. My father had mentioned her in one of his
letters to me, but I didn't think seriously of her until I
met her.

'May I dance with you?' I asked her bowing low. She got
up quickly. 'Of course,' she said in a very sweet voice, the
sweetest I have ever heard. And my experience in my first
year in London at a Nigerian dance came back vividly to me:
I had asked a Nigerian girl for a dance. She surveyed me
from head to toe, and threw away her face muttering in a
Nigerian language which I did not understand.

It was a high life, so we were able to talk. 'You are Mr.
Ogun?' she asked.

'Yes, and you are Miss Gobi,' I said.

'You know me?' she said.

'Of course. I have heard so much about you,' I said.

'Really. Now, what and what have you heard about me?'
she asked.

'Let's not talk about that now. When did you arrive
London?'

'If you wish. Three months ago.'

We danced and we talked. I was beginning to like her. She
was so cheerful and easy. She was not inhibited in any way.
She told me she was enjoying her course. In fact she had
made friends with some English girls in her class, and they
had invited her to their homes. When you know them, you
like them, she said.

21

I didn't want to tell her about my own experience in my University. I wanted her to find out things for herself. I must give her a chance. If she found some of her class girls nice, all well and good.

She told me she knew my younger sister. They were at school together, and she had seen my photographs in her album. My younger sister was fond of me, too fond of me in fact. She had ideas about the girl friends I should have, and proceeded to choose them for me. It amused me greatly. I let her do it to humour her. When she was tired of seeing them in my company, she recommended their sack. Miss Gobi knew this, and avoided her company at school, because there were always gossips about the girls and I. She came to dance with her brother. And I knew that if I were to get on well with her, I had to make his acquaintance. So after the dance, I took her back to her brother, then to the bar and bought drinks for them.

Rose and I got married in London. It was a quiet wedding. I would have wanted a noisy wedding if I could afford it. We invited six guests including the best man and the bridesmaid. Two months after our wedding, I returned home and left Rose in London. She took my departure calmly. For days, I knew it bothered her, but she was a calm girl by nature and she bore it very well.

In the boat I met Maria. She was a glamour girl. You simply saw glamour written on her forehead. She carried a very large wig on her head. The make-up was revolting. But she was irresistible. She was every inch a woman. Very. feminine. I fell for her. I fell for her make-up, I fell for her wig, I fell for her wiggle. All the qualities she possessed, including her make-up were what I told my wife I abhorred in women. And here was I.

I thought that the affair would end in the boat, but I was mistaken. It did not. Maria stuck like a leech. At Apapa wharf, she introduced me to every member of her family who came to welcome her. She invited me to her home the next day.

22

She embarrassed me greatly. Rose's relatives were there and my two cousins and childhood friend, Asare, were there as well. But I thought I handled the situation well.

I was staying with Asare. He was a civil servant and lived in Ikoyi. I was going to be a civil servant also, but I did not want to live in Ikoyi. I persuaded Asare to take me to Maria's place the next day. He did.

The welcome was tumultuous. We drank and we ate. The merrymaking started the day of our arrival and continued the following day. There were four juju bands, and each tried to outplay the others. The drinks flowed. We did not leave until in the early hours of the morning. We were there at eight o'clock in the evening.

I travelled home to see my parents before I assumed duty in Lagos. They did not want me to work in Lagos. They wanted me near home. The troubles of home people would weary me and make life unbearable. There was nothing they could do, so I returned to Lagos.

Maria got a job in one of the Ministries. We were in the same building. I don't know whether I liked this or not. I thought she was going to work at Ibadan. I wondered whether it was because of me that she changed her mind. She definitely told me in the boat that she was going to work at Ibadan. This worried me a bit. I hadn't told her I was married. She hadn't asked.

I wasn't in love with Maria. I was merely attracted to her. She was becoming possessive. Then one day, she behaved in a way that convinced me that she was not normal. I had gone to her flat. We went to Kakadu to dance. For days she had told me she wanted to go to Kakadu. So I took her there on a Saturday. We danced for a little while. I asked a girl to dance with me, while a friend danced with Maria. When the music stopped I took the girl to her seat. Maria was already seated. She stood up and demanded that we must go.

'Wait a little, dear. What is wrong?'

'We must go now. I am sick of this place,' she said. She had never behaved in that way before. Maria was a quiet girl. She

23

was glamorous but she did not talk much. Her behaviour surprised me. Before I could persuade her, she was making for the door. I followed her.

I wanted to drive her to my flat, but she protested. She said she wanted to go home. She didn't want to sleep with me that night. I drove her home. In her flat she removed her dress, and dumped it in the sink. Her wig, she also dumped in the sink. I drove her to the hairdresser that afternoon to collect the wig. 'What is the matter?' I asked her, holding her hands. I tried to be as calm as possible, though I was afraid.

'We are married, aren't we? And we have two children, haven't we?'

Up till now, I cannot remember how I left Maria's flat, and how I drove my car home. It was about midnight when I arrived home. Two single girls shared a flat in the block. They were above me. Both girls held good jobs, both had cars and a string of men friends. As I was parking my car, one of them came out from a taxi. She was dead drunk. She shouted my name as she staggered up the stairs. I came rushing to her. I piloted her to her flat. The words Maria said were still ringing in my ears.

'Where are you coming from, you are so drunk?' I asked.

'Never mind where I am coming from. I went out. I am drunk. I am so drunk. I must tell you, stop that girl from coming to your flat, Jide. I knew her in London. Stop seeing her. Oh I am so drunk. Take me to my room. Iyabo is not back. Perhaps she will come home drunk like myself. You know Jide, there is nothing like getting drunk. Have you ever been drunk?' she asked me.

'Yes,' I said. But my mind was on Maria and what she said. 'We are married and we have two children?' Perhaps Maria was drunk. No. She was not. She did not drink. I remember I forced her to drink brandy and ginger in the boat, and it nearly choked her. She drank only soft drinks. Then I heard Peju again. She was now lying on the sofa in the living room which she shared with her friend, Iayabo.

'I'll tell you about her. Ask me. I was saying, if you hadn't

24

been drunk, then you haven't started living. To be able to live, you have to get drunk, really drunk. Have you ever been drunk on stout?'

'I have to go now,' I said and got up.

'It's bad to get drunk. When you get drunk on stout, for days you are drunk. You move as if in a dream. Try it. Jide, I am drunk. But you heard me. Look for another girl friend. Sack her. I can't be your girl friend. Iyabo can't be either. You can't afford us. You see this bracelet? It cost one hundred and twenty pounds. How much do you earn? How much . . .'

She was asleep. I closed the door quietly. I went downstairs to my room. Just as I was inserting the key in the keyhole, Maria appeared. I don't know how I did it, but I carried her into my car. She did not resist. I carried her into her bedroom, locked her in and drove home.

I went upstairs to Peju. That was the second time I was in their flat. The first time was last night. She was up already and in the kitchen. She looked as calm as the lagoon after a storm. She hadn't had her bath. She was in her dressing gown. And she was chewing chewing-stick. She went to the sink and spat out a mouthful of reddish stuff, and washed her mouth before she came out.

'You must stay for breakfast. I am cooking *moi-moi*.'

I sat down. I was in my dressing gown too. I watched her. Was this the lady who was so drunk last night?

'Where is Iyabo?' I asked.

'Still sleeping. I'll wake her up when I finish cooking breakfast. Lazy girl. she can't cook,' Peju said

She went back to the kitchen. I sat in the living room reading Sunday papers. I wasn't interested in what I was reading. I came up to hear what Peju had to say about Maria. I wanted to know everything. Rose would soon be back, and I had to clear everything before she returned. I disliked this kind of mess. Maria wasn't a bad girl, but certainly something was wrong.

Iyabo came out in a dressing gown. She was still half

25

asleep, and a bit drunk. 'Jide, good morning,' she said. 'I was drunk last night. Really tight last night.'

'You came home after Peju then?'

'I came home after her. Peju, are you ready?'

'You mean is breakfast ready? Never mind. Your turn next Sunday. I don't want to eat raw *moi-moi* next Sunday,' Peju shouted from the kitchen.

The *moi-moi* was steaming hot. There were some gari in water and ogi. It was the most delicious *moi-moi* I have ever eaten. 'I didn't know you knew how to cook so well,' I said for want of anything to say.

'You couldn't have known without tasting my cooking,' she said. Iyabo was eating seriously. I envied her appetite. I had no appetite for food that morning.

The maid brought some tea in large bowls, and milk and sugar. We drank the tea as we ate the *moi-moi*.

'I know why you are here,' Peju said to me.

'Why is he here?' Iyabo asked obviously not interested in the answer.

'He has come to know about Maria,' Peju said.

'Maria, oh. I know,' and she laughed. It was a mocking sort of laugh. She finished eating, announced that she was going back to bed and left us.

The maid cleared the table and I sat down. Peju sat down opposite me. 'I didn't know you would recollect what you said last night when you were drunk,' I said.

She smiled. 'I shouldn't get drunk,' she said. 'But somehow I can't help it at times. I didn't drink in England at all. I started drinking two years after my return. Things were not as they seemed. And now it seems as if I am beyond redemption. Don't preach to me. I know you drink too. You would say that it is not good for a woman to drink and all that. If it is good for a man I wonder why it is not for a woman. I was driven to it, and now, I can't stop.'

'The other night I was so drunk I nearly killed myself,' I said.

'Don't ever drive when you are drunk,' she said. 'Last week,' she went on, 'I went to Ibadan. I knew I was going to get drunk there, so I went in a taxi. I got a lift back. The man was going to catch a plane at Ikeja. He was doing over one hundred m.p.h. I begged him to drive slowly, that I did not like speed, that I had my mother to bury, but the man said that he would miss the plane if he did not speed. So I asked him to stop, that I wanted to ease myself. He stopped. I took my bag, and I waved to him. "Safe journey," I said. He moved on. He was in fact in a hurry. I saw one of these big buses. I waved. It stopped and I entered. The passengers stared at me. I had my sunglasses on. So they did not see me staring back at them. It stopped at the Yaba Roundabout. I took a taxi home.'

'Have something to drink,' she said when she finished her story.

'No, thanks,' I said. 'Tell me about Maria.'

'Maria, poor girl. It wasn't her fault. Men, they doom we women. Very intelligent girl. And I hear that she handles her job in the Ministry very well. So they can't sack her, and of course, she has connections, and you wouldn't really know she is not well.'

'Is she insane?' I asked gripping the chair.

'She is insane. She went off her head in London. She was in the asylum for nearly a year. But being a brilliant girl, she was able to finish her course before she returned. Her husband was cruel to her so it entered her head. Her two sons are still in London.'

'She has two sons?'

'Two sons,' she said. That explained it. 'We are married aren't we, and we have two children, haven't we?'

Maria's husband locked her up several days in their flat in London without food. He beat her and he gave her no money for her and her children. The cruelty went into her head as Peju said. Before her mother came, she was already in the asylum. Her two boys were with her mother in London. The psychiatrist believed that Maria would be better if she left

27

London. Certain things like the weather and scenes reminded her of the cruelty of her husband, and made her case worse. Maria did not behave queerly until yesterday. The whole thing was coming up again. What could I do? I had to make myself scarce, especially as my wife would be due back in a few weeks.

Rose wrote regularly every week. Whether I wrote or not, she was sure to write every Sunday. It was sweet of her. She gave an account of what she did in the week and any exciting persons she met. She was good at letter writing. I wasn't.

In the office on Monday, Maria telephoned. She sounded sane. She hoped I had an enjoyable weekend. She hung up. In a few minutes, she rang again, then again and again. At this rate she would not allow me to work. I put the receiver of the telephone on my table. Then I feared that she would decide to come upstairs to my office. I replaced the receiver. She did not ring again.

For a fortnight I did not see Maria. She did not telephone, she didn't visit. That was a good sign. She would leave me alone. I hadn't anything against Maria. She was a nice girl. If she hadn't behaved in the way she did, I would never have believed Peju. She still dressed loudly, still carried her wig instead of wearing it, still was competent in her job. I wondered how she did it.

In the next week or two, I was engaged in arranging the reception of my wife. She was returning by boat. Perhaps she would meet someone in the boat who would like to sleep with her as I slept with Maria, I thought. The thought was unfair to my wife. She had given me no cause whatever to think this thought. She was not a virgin of course, but it was unfair to her.

So on a Saturday, I went to Kakadu, got drunk, really drunk and took a woman to my house for the night. That was the first time I did it. I had other casual girl friends in the Ministries besides Maria. But that morning, I took a prostitute home.

I saw myself doing that every day of the week until the

arrival of my wife. I shocked myself. Asare, my good friend, was horrified, but he could do nothing about it.

At last, Rose returned. How nice it was to have her back. She hadn't changed a bit. Simple and fresh. No make-up. Not even a lipstick. I told her in London I didn't like wigs and lipsticks.

My friends were invited, and we had a wonderful time. The two girls, Peju and Iyabo were there. They arranged for a juju band in spite of my protests. Their men friends came in their long cars and brought drinks. My wife enjoyed it all, though she complained that I was extravagant.

After the merriments, she went home to see her parents, just as I did when I returned. I was surprised to see myself still going to Kakadu and bringing women home.

When Rose returned, I didn't want to take her to Kakadu. I took her to other night clubs. She insisted, and so I took her there. We did not quite settle down when two ladies came. 'Hello darling, hello darling,' they said. I got up quickly. 'Please sit down,' I said. I didn't know what else to say. I knew the two ladies all right. One of them had spent many nights with me before my wife returned. They looked at my wife. She smiled in a superior sort of way. 'Please make yourselves comfortable,' I said. They looked at my wife again. They declined and went away.

I sat down. I looked at my wife. She wasn't looking at me. She was watching the dancers on the floor. 'Let's dance,' I said. She got up and I followed her. We danced high life. We did not talk. It was so strange. Why didn't we say anything to each other?

I drank a beer. She wanted a gin and tonic. That was rather sophisticated. I got it for her. Then it came to me. That was the first time she had asked for gin and tonic. Not even when I was courting her. We drank in silence. The band began to play again. I wanted to dance with abandonment. But Rose danced in a refined sort of way which I did not like. 'I'll take you to Federal Palace Hotel, there you can dance waltz,' I said. 'Nobody dances waltz in Nigeria these days.'

'Don't I dance high life well?' she asked. 'You do. But you don't seem to enjoy it,' I said. 'I enjoy it,' she said.

After that night, my wife did not mention Kakadu again, neither did she ask questions about the ladies. I went alone and I enjoyed myself. To further kill her interest in night clubs, I took her to Lido. We did not sit for an hour when she said we must go. We left. I tucked her nicely in bed and went out again.

I arrived at Kakadu at midnight. Arinze and his boys were blasting away. The place was boiling hot. I joined a group of friends and we made merry.

Then Herbert came and joined us. He worked in the Ministry with me. We drank and drank. I asked a lady for a dance. She was a prostitute from the way she danced and behaved. We danced. She danced with complete abandonment. That was what I wanted. I danced and drank. Then blackout.

I woke up. I looked at my watch. It was nine in the morning I slapped my forehead, attempting to understand. The room was strange. The bed was stange. Then a voice: 'Are you up darling?' No. What voice is that? Whose voice is that? 'Are you up darling?' she asked again, perhaps thinking I was not up. That's not Rose's voice? The room, the strange bed, the strange woman. What happened? Herbert? Kakadu? 'Am up,' I said. 'I'll bring you water to wash your face,' she said. 'Won't you wash your face?' she asked. 'I'll wash my face,' I said getting up. 'I'll wash my face all right. But tell me, where am I?' 'You are in my house. You are in Angelina's house,' she said. Angelina, Angelina. I could not recollect. Names like Maria, Rose, Peju, Bisi, Iyabo, Comfort, etc., made sense. Not Angelina. Rose, what will Rose think? Did she sleep at all? Had she gone to call the police? Her husband did not return the night before. She must have gone to call the police. The instruction I gave her when she first returned from London was to go to Asare if she was in any trouble and I was not available. Perhaps she went to Asare, and they were looking for me. And I am here.

Angelina looked at my face. 'This is your car key. This is your wallet. It dropped last night, and I picked it up. Your car is outside. You can go if you like.' The car. Of course. I drove my car to Kakadu last night. Yes, Herbert was saying something about driving me home. 'Thank you very much,' I said. I picked the car key on the table and my wallet. Angelina watched me go.

I could not recollect my bearing. From the smell, I knew that I was in the heart of Lagos, on a Sunday morning. Children came out to wave as I drove away.

As I drove along, my bearing came back to me. I knew where I was. Yes, here was the Reclamation Road. That was right. Soon I was on the Carter Bridge. For no reason at all, I took the Ijora Causeway. Then I saw Asare's car. The time was nine thirty. I slowed down, and stopped.

Rose was sitting in front of Asare's car. She had the Sunday papers on her lap. She was still crying. Then Asare came out. 'Jide, no. What is this?' My wife said nothing. All I saw on her face was relief. 'I had trouble with my car last night,' I stammmered. I gave Asare a look.

Asare turned back. He went back to the Police Station. Then he came back. Rose came into my car and we drove home.

I had a bath. Asare stayed for breakfast. We ate and I went back to bed. For days I stayed home. Rose did not ask the simple question, 'Where did you sleep?' If she had asked, perhaps it would have been better. I would have felt better and less guilty. Was Rose up to something? Didn't she love me? Was she having an affair? Why did she not ask questions? We have no child yet. Was this worrying her?

For a week, I did not go out. I would come home, eat, sleep, go to bed, wake up, watch television and go back to bed again. It was in this week that I saw how busy my wife was. She cooked, cleaned and mended. The servant was constantly kept busy. She was a dutiful wife.

But I had to go out. It wasn't easy staying home all the time. And besides, I was spending far too much money on

31

drinks. A friend would drop in, we split a bottle of beer. Then another would drop in again, another beer.

So on a Saturday night, I went out. It was a house party, not many people and good company. I didn't drink much. It was a party I really enjoyed. I met many interesting people. We talked. Friends wanted us to go to Kakadu. I did not feel like it. It was only midnight, and I decided to go home. It was unusual for me on a Saturday night.

'Your sister has arrived from home. The door was locked, so she is waiting there,' the night watchman said, pointing at a figure in front of me. It was Maria. She had on a long black dress. 'I am ready,' she said.

'Ready for what?' I asked.

'Aren't we going to London to collect the two kids?' she said.

'Please, please go home.'

'I won't go home. You promised we were going to London tomorrow. I won't go home. I just won't go home,' she started shouting. 'You promised in writing. Here are the letters you wrote, you did. The letters are in this bag.'

It was past midnight, but a crowd gathered. I had no words. Then one from the crowd spoke up, 'Look woman, go home. He doesn't want you.' 'Asawo' another called from the crowd. And they started jeering at her.

Then a taxi stopped. It was Iyabo. She was drunk of course. 'Taxi, take her, take the mad woman away,' one in the crowd said. The taxi driver hooted. 'You no go go?' the man from the crowd said. The taxi driver hooted again. 'Oya,' he said.

I stood. I was so embarrassed and helpless. If the crowd could persuade her to go, all well and good. The noise was much and I was afraid my wife would hear.

The next thing I saw was that somebody in the crowd had collected Maria as you would collect a baby to fondle her, and put her in the taxi. 'Taxi, oya. Take her to her home. And you, woman, don't come here again. The man no want you.'

I climbed upstairs. I entered the bedroom. My wife was fast asleep. I couldn't wait. 'Rose,' I called gently. 'I know you heard,' I said. 'Heard what?' she asked. She was not pretending. She did not hear. She got up and rubbed her eyes. 'The crowd and the woman who was waiting for me.' 'You mean she did not go?' she asked. 'Did you know she was here?' It was my turn to be surprised. She smiled in a sad way. 'She came here as soon as you left. I heard a knock, so I opened the door, and said, come in. She came in. I said, "Sit down." She sat down. Then she said, "Are you not ashamed of yourself? Are you not ashamed of yourself living with a man who doesn't love you? Jide is my husband. We were married in Brighton and we have two children." I got up, went to my room and locked the door. After an hour or so, I came out and she was gone. So she was waiting for you. You returned early tonight. Do you want to eat something?'

For days I thought Rose would ask questions, but she did not. What was at the back of her mind? Was she being liberal? Did she love me at all? Why was she not jealous? Why did she behave in that superior manner? Was she making a fool of me? I was told that when a married woman had affairs with men, it was her husband who was the last to know.

I became very jealous. I began suspecting every man that came to our house, even my friends. But it was no good. Rose was elusive. She did not show indifference. She was loving, but I just could not predict her. She showed me love and care, but I could not reach her. There was something between us, a barrier. It was solidly there. Did she know it? Was she fooling me? I could never know.

# The Road to Benin

Nwanyimma lived with her husband at Onitsha. They had four children. Her husband was a daily paid labourer. For years, he was daily paid. That meant that when he was ill, he was not paid. And he was nearly always ill, and his wife could not understand why he was so ill. He was such a strong man when they were married. Of course that was a long time ago.

Nwanyimma traded in fruits and all kinds of vegetables. She had white women as her customers. She did not go to school, but she was able to speak pidgin English which the white women were able to speak as well. She did not only sell to white women, she also sold to cooks of white men. Thus she was in a very privileged position. Her customers were those who were able to pay any price. She did not cheat them, she had the best and sold them to her customers. When she had bad carrots or onions, she persuaded her customers to go elsewhere. Or she went and bought the things she did not have for her customers.

Two of their children were in school. The eldest showed great promise. He topped the class every examination, and how to send him to a secondary or a technical school was already occupying the minds of Nwanyimma and her husband. They were determined to do their best. They would ask for help in the church, they would enter into any bond to make it possible for their son to go to college. The only thing they knew they were not going to do, was go to a money lender. They would be ruined if they went to one of the numerous ones in Onitsha.

In the boy's final year, Nwanyimma discovered that the boy spent less time at home and more outside. She told her husband. 'I have noticed it too,' her husband said, 'but I don't think it should cost us sleepless nights. The boy still does well at school. Let's not worry about this.'

Nwanyimma agreed with her husband. Perhaps he was right. Women saw these things first. Well, maybe she was being anxious for nothing. Her son was growing up and growing up has so many difficulties.

One day when Nwanyimma returned from the market, she saw her son's teacher in their house. She put down her load quickly and went to greet him. 'It is nice of you to come and see us today. Have you been here long?' 'No, I have just come.' 'Sit down and let's find you some kola. Oh my husband is not back yet.' 'He is back. He has just gone out. Actually he asked me to sit down and wait for you.'

Nwanyimma went into the room, washed a kola, put it in a kola dish and brought it before the teacher. While they were having the kola, the maid brought a large bottle of stout, and placed it before the teacher. 'All these troubles. You shouldn't go into this expense,' the teacher said, opening the stout. 'Please take it like that. It is not always that one sees the teacher of one's son in one's house. This is a busy time for you. The children have just done their exams.' 'Very busy time indeed, very busy time indeed,' the teacher said, drinking his stout with relish. Nwanyimma's husband came in and sat down. 'Let me bring you a glass,' Nwanyimma said to her husband. 'That won't be bad at all,' her husband said taking the kola from the kola dish. He poured himself some stout and drank, with relish like the teacher.

'I have come to tell you about Ezeka,' the teacher said. Nwanyimma's heart missed a beat. She shifted uncomfortably in her chair. She looked intently at her husband, then at the teacher, who had emptied the bottle of stout and was drinking greedily. He saw the anxiety on the faces of his host and hostess. 'Is it well?' Nwanyimma asked. Her husband said nothing. He just stared. 'It is very well. Ezeka passed the

35

entrance to Umuahia Government College and he won a scholarship, and . . .'

Nwanyimma jumped up. 'Ezeka my son, my son, a scholarship. No.' She gripped her husband who sat where he was, like a man, solid, no excesses. 'Tell us more.' 'He is the only child in the school who passed. All the others failed. So I have come to congratulate you.'

Nwanyimma called the maid and asked her to get two more bottles of stout. She shouted to her neighbour to come and hear good news. She came and Nwanyimma told her. She jumped up. She was happy for her. She ran out and told everybody on the compound.

'And you came in as if you brought bad news,' she said to the teacher. 'You people who went to school, you have a way of restraining yourselves. See how my husband just sits there. He is so happy, but he does not show it. And only a few weeks ago we were anxious about our boy. You were right my husband, you were right. You said we shouldn't be so anxious about our son's bad habits of not staying at home. A good thing we did not make any fuss.' The maid brought the two bottles of stout and the men began to drink. 'That means that we are not going to pay for his education, that the Government is going to pay for everything,' Nwanyimma said. 'Exactly,' the teacher said. 'You know when you entered, I thought Ezeka had done something bad, and you had come to tell us. But where is he? Where is the lucky boy? We will celebrate today.' She called the maid and asked her to kill the chicken at the back of the house. She would use it to cook a delicious food for Ezeka to eat. 'Won't you join us?' she asked the teacher. 'No, thank you all the same. I have had stout. I must be going now. Congratulate your son for me, and ask him to come and take the details from the Headmaster tomorrow.'


Ezeka returned on holiday. It was his first term holiday. His mother was surprised that he had grown so tall. She

36

wondered what made boys grow very tall when they left their parents. He was no longer the little boy she used to send on errands. She discovered that before she had the courage to ask him to do anything for her, she had to think twice about it. The old days were gone when she called him, sometimes roughly, and asked him to do this, or do that.

There was also a lot of change. Nwanyimma could see the boredom on Ezeka's face when he was at home. At first it worried her, but later on, she attributed it again to the difficulties of growing up. There was no sense in worrying about her son. The school would take care of him. She had done her duty to her son. Now in a way, she had handed over her son to the authorities of the school. It was the authority that she trusted and respected. She had no fear whatever.

Nwanyimma was always delighted to see Ezeka's school friends in the house when she returned home from the market. She gave them whatever she bought. One day she was surprised to hear Ezeka ask her to get some beer for his friends. She refused. 'Beer, my child, when you are in school? They don't allow you to drink beer at school. Why should I get beer for you? No my child. I bought groundnuts, pears and corn. The maid can roast the corn and some pears for you. 'Let's go out,' Ezeka said to his friends. 'We shall go and drink somewhere.'

Nwanyimma did not eat that day. She told her husband when he returned. 'What is Ezeka turning into?' 'You should have given him the beer,' her husband said. 'Give him beer? What are you talking about? A schoolboy? I should buy beer for my son and his friends? Oh no.' 'He had beer outside. You said he went out immediately. He went out to have beer elsewhere with his friends. Whereas if he had had beer here, he wouldn't have gone out. Don't you understand what I am saying?' 'I am surprised. I understand all right. I am only surprised. I am not going to buy beer for Ezeka. Let it be clear to you and to him. How much does a bottle of beer cost? Do you think we can afford that luxury? I sell vegetables and fruits in the market you know. And you are a labourer. Does Ezeka think we can afford beer in that way? Even if we could afford it, must we give him beer at this stage? You are talking rubbish. My son cannot dictate to me in my own house, because he is at college. Oh no.'

Ezeka became more aloof every day of the holiday. He was becoming quite a problem. He came in late and woke up when his parents had gone to work. He lorded it over his brother and the two sisters. He ordered them about, and they complained to their mother each time she returned from the market. When his mother talked to him, he did not listen. What was she going to do? What had gone wrong with Ezeka?

Ezeka went out one morning with his friends. His mother had gone to the market. These friends were not his school friends as his mother believed. They were loafers of Onitsha. They had nothing to do, and Ezeka discovered them even before he went to Umuahia Government College.

They went to a place where they ate 'suya' and drank palm wine. Then someone suggested that they should go to a bar at Asaba. There was nothing in particular they were going to do there. It was mere youthfulness. They could either go by taxi or by one of the numerous launches that plied Asaba and Onitsha. They decided to go by launch. None of them knew how to swim, but it did not matter. The launches were well built, they were going in one of them, and not in a canoe. Ezeka wouldn't have gone with them if they were going in a canoe.

At Asaba they went to a bar, and the boys called for some drinks and 'suya'. The bar attendant brought beer and 'suya' for them. She looked at them and shook her head. She knew that they had no business to be there, but she could not ask them to leave the bar. Traders poured into the bar, looked at the boys and shook their heads. One in particular could bear it no longer, so he said to the boys, 'Come, my children, what are you doing here? Did you tell your mothers before you came here? Don't you know that children don't come here. If you don't leave this minute,

I shall call the police "omesie unu ike".'

The boys were frightened. 'What is Nigeria turning into?' the trader said to the others. 'Look at these children coming here to drink beer and eat 'suya'. Out you go before I call the police.'

The boys trooped out. The trader watched them menacingly.

'Ewoo, come. You are the son of Nwanyimma?' he asked Ezeka.

'I am not,' Ezeka spoke in English. The trader had been speaking to them in Ibo. 'You are Nwanyimma's son who is at college. I know your mother very well. And you, a boy at college in the company of these never do wells. I am going to tell your mother.' He turned to the other customers, and said, 'I know his mother, a good woman. We all rejoiced with her when she told us that her son had not only passed the entrance to college, but that he had won a scholarship. A good woman. And here is the son in this bar.'

'It is her fault for not looking after her son well,' a trader said.

'She spends all her time in the market. So she should tie her son on to her cloth, so he would be a good son. What are you talking about? You people just talk rubbish at times.'

'It is enough,' the trader said. 'I say it is enough.'

The trader who said he knew Ezeka's mother said, 'It is enough. I should say that to you. Next time don't put your mouth into something you don't know about. You merely make yourself ridiculous.'

'Di anyi ozugo,' another trader said. The trader who knew Nwanyimma drank up his beer and walked out of the bar. There was no point staying there. He was too big to fight in a bar. He would get home. The next day, he would go to Nwanyimma in her stall and tell her about her son.

When he arrived home, he could not wait. So he went straight to Nwanyimma. She was not at home. The children were sitting idly and sad.

'Where is your mother?' he asked.

'She is not in,' the boy said.

'Where has she gone to? And your father, isn't he in as well?'

'He has gone out with mother. Nwanyimma's other son, Ezeka, has been missing since morning, so they have gone out to find him,' the youngest child said.

'Keep quiet, Nkiru,' the boy said. 'Nobody asked you to say anything.'

The child melted away. 'My mother and father went out,' the boy said.

'Thank you very much,' the trader said and left.

On his way home, he met Nwanyimma and her husband. 'I am from your house, and . . .' He did not finish. He saw Nwanyimma's face.

'It is Ezeka. He has not come home since morning. We have been to all the places he used to go to, but nobody knew where he went. He has not been all that good of late, but he always returned home to eat and then went out again. His afternoon food is there and so is his evening meal. Where can he be?'

'I saw him at Asaba,' the trader said.

'Asaba?' Nwanyimma and her husband asked almost simultaneously.

'Yes, Asaba. I did not like the company he had. They were in a bar when I came in. So I drove them out of the place. I said I would tell you the next day, but when I returned and had my bath, I came right away. I didn't like the company at all, a boy who is at school, and a good school at that. So he has not returned?'

'He has not returned,' Nwanyimma said.

'You better report to the police,' the trader said.

'They say we should not report to the police as yet, because if we did, his school might hear of it and suspend him from school, or even dismiss him.'

'Well, I don't know about that, Nwanyimma, but it is better for you to find your son and let his school suspend him than not find your son at all.'

40

'I think he is right. Let's go and report to the police,' Nwanyimma said.

'Let's go to Asaba first,' her husband said.

'This night? Where do you think we can find him this night at Asaba? Let's go to the police.'

So they went to the police. They gave all particulars, mentioning that a friend saw him and a group of boys at Asaba in the afternoon. The policeman was kind and sympathetic. He telephoned Asaba Police Station and asked whether there were some boys in the cell. There were no boys there.

'I am sure that if Ezeka is alive, he must return home. He is dead, that's why he has not returned home to us. Please don't say that.' Nwanyimma's husband was more afraid than Nwanyimma herself. His heart was breaking. He wished he could cry like Nwanyimma, so he would feel better.

'We shall bring you word tomorrow,' the policeman said. 'Or better still, call in this office tomorrow.'

'Ewoo o ka nsi je?' Nwanyimma wept. Sympathisers poured in. Nobody seemed to know the boys who went out with Ezeka. Those who usually went out with him were all home with their parents. He had no time for those who were in school with him at the central school. In his opinion, he had left them far behind, and he had nothing in common anymore with them.

The next morning brought no news. So they decided to go to Asaba. They took a launch and crossed to the other side, it was cheaper and quicker for people going to Asaba to still go by launch. The Niger Bridge was for those who owned cars, not for the common people.

Nwanyimma and her husband and the good trader went to the bar where Ezeka and the others had drinks the previous day. The trader suggested that they should go there. If there was an accident or something the people in the bar would know about it and talk about it.

As soon as they entered, the girl who served the boys the previous day came in to take the orders. When she brought

stout to them, the trader beckoned her to come to him. She
went. 'You remember those boys who were here yesterday?'
The girl shook her head. It was not easy for her to remember.
They have a hundred and one customers every day. It was a
popular bar.

'Do you remember me? I came here yesterday. You served
me beer here yesterday.'

'Yes, I remember you,' the girl said. She was smiling now.
She thought that the man liked her and wanted a date with her.

'Good. I came here yesterday. I saw a group of four boys
here yesterday and I scolded them. Do you remember?'

She shook her head. 'I served you and went away. I didn't
see the boys.'

'No you were here when I was scolding the boys. You
stood there and . . .'

'What is it "di anyi, onwe ife gaa"?'

'No, we are merely trying to locate the whereabouts of a
boy who was here yesterday with three other boys,' the good
trader said.

'And does she say that she does not remember them?' the
owner of the bar said.

'Come, Grace, don't you remember the boys you served
yesterday? She served them here yesterday. She should
remember.' The girl nodded.

'Good. Do you know where they went?' Nwanyimma
asked.

'Woman, how can we know where they went. They came
here, were served and they left.'

'You didn't hear of an accident yesterday at Asaba?'
Ezeka's father asked.

'No. Call Michael,' the owner of the bar said. Michael
came.

'Did you hear of any accidents yesterday or today at
Asaba?'

'No sir,' Michael replied. The bar owner shrugged his
shoulders and went to attend to fresh customers who had
just come in.

42

Nwanyimma and her husband and the trader sat down unable to make up their minds what to do next. The trader suggested they should stay there a little while. There was no point roaming about the streets of Asaba as if Ezeka would be found walking along the street. But he himself went out, and did not come back until after almost two hours. Nwanyimma and her husband just sat there and waited. Her husband did not go to work that day. It meant that he was not going to be paid for that day, but what did it matter. How could they be so lucky in the beginning and suddenly become unlucky. It was not often these days, colonial days, yes, but not these days, that the son of a labourer gained admission into such a school as Government College, Umuahia. Why was this sudden light, which had illuminated his poor family which had been in the dark all these years, suddenly turn into darkness? They thought that the light was going to burn forever. It was not the kind of light that was easily extinguished. It was difficult for it to enter in the first place into your household, but once it gained entrance it remained there forever. Who was extinguishing the light? An enemy? Fate? If it were fate, what brought it in, in the first place? It was not easy to comprehend. For simple folks like Nwanyimma and her husband it was mysterious.

Nwanyimma was getting tired of staying in the bar when two people entered. They were tired, and they asked for cold beer each. Each emptied his bottle in the twinkle of an eye, and asked for more. Then they went and sat down. 'That's the only way to enjoy beer when you are tired and thirsty. Drink a whole bottle in a gulp and then sip a second. It goes down to the right places in your body and cools you,' one told the other. Those in the bar laughed. In spite of all Nwanyimma could not help smiling.

'I went to court,' the same man said.

'Which court?'

'Benin magistrate's court.'

'So when I saw you at the petrol station at Benin you were just from the court?'

43

'Yes.'

'About that case?'

'Yes, about that case. I have everything in control. I told them. They are going to squash the case.'

'What happened?'

'The case was adjourned.'

'Again?'

'Everything is working according to plan. Shake my hand. We control this country. Everything is working according to plan. I am going again next month. It will be ajourned again. I told them. More beer please, waiter,' he shouted, and the waiter came with two bottles of beer. 'Don't go away. Here is your money. I'll have another before I go though. I don't want to eat. I don't feel like eating anything. And what did I see today at Benin Magistrate's Court? Two children convicted of being in possession of "we we".' The glass fell from Nwanyimma's hand. Her husband held her. The good trader stared at husband and wife, then recovered quickly and went over to the man.

'Please, don't be annoyed. Tell me about the boys who were convicted at Benin Magistrate's Court. Shall we go outside?'

The man was at first aggressive. 'You want me to leave my drink and come with you? Why not wait and hear the whole story?'

'No. You see those people over there, they are looking for their son. He was here yesterday and since then nobody knows where he is. And you mentioned two boys and "we we". One of them could be this woman's son.'

'Are you the husband?'

'No, that's the husband next to her, holding her. I am only a friend.'

'I am sorry. Let's go and talk outside.'

The case was treated as an overnight case. The boys pleaded guilty, and the magistrate convicted them. 'Something must be done,' Nwanyimma said. 'I have to see my son first. "We we", my son? Impossible. I'll see him with my own eyes first. What happened exactly?'

It was said that the boys saw a taxi driver who said he was going to Benin. The boys asked if they could go with him. The taxi driver agreed. At Agbor, police searched the taxi and some Indian hemp was discovered under the seat. The taxi driver 'confessed' that the boys hired him. They were all locked up in the cell. The next morning, they appeared in court. The taxi driver was prosecution witness, and the two boys were jailed. The other two boys refused to go to Benin. They had more exciting places to go to.

At first, Nwanyimma refused to believe that one of the children jailed was Ezeka. She hoped that one day her son would return, but after nearly a week when Ezeka did not return, they decided to go to the prison at Benin.

They did not know anybody. Nwanyimma went to the trader who took them to the man who told them of the case at Benin. 'It will cost money,' he said to them. 'How much do you think you can afford?' 'How much will they take? All we want to do is go to the prison and see whether our son is there. That's all,' Nwanyimma explained. 'I know. It costs money.' 'I have to pay to go and visit my son in prison?' Nwanyimma asked. 'Nothing goes for nothing. You pay for everything in Nigeria these days. I would have been in jail if I didn't pay. You see my point?' Nwanyimma's husband nodded. He got his job before independence and he had not changed it. He had never given bribe to anybody, and he had always been a daily paid labourer. 'Bring ten pounds. I shall beg them with ten pounds. Can you afford that?'

'We shall go home and look for ten pounds.'

'Can you borrow? I know a money lender who can lend you ten pounds on easy terms.'

'We won't borrow from a money lender,' Nwanyimma's husband said.

The money was got. Nwanyimma and her husband arrived at Benin. The man took them to a house at night and introduced them to a hefty man, who was most unceremonious. 'Come to the prisons at eleven o'clock tomorrow.

There is a boy, but I don't know his name. He is not actually in prison, as he is not an adult. I'll show him to you when you come.'

The next day, they were at the prisons at ten o'clock. They did not want to take chances. They were there until four o'clock when someone asked them their names, and when they told him, he asked them in.

Ezeka stared at his parents. They were able to recognise him because he was their son. Otherwise he was so different from what he looked over seven days ago. 'Thank God you are alive. What happened? Tell us.' Ezeka stared back. 'Can you talk?' His mother shook him. He stared back. His eyes were red. He looked like an imbecile. He did not just look it. He was one.

Nwanyimma held on to her husband. Her husband carried her weight sort of. His body was weak. He had known hard work all his life. He did not mind cutting the grass in the DO's house or around his office. He could get on well with that. Not this. Not this kind of weight, that seemed to crush him.

They stared at their son. They were also as dumb as their son. Time was passing. They were not aware of it. They were warned that they had a few minutes to stay with him. Soon it would be time. 'What happened?' Nwanyimma's husband managed to say. No answer came.

Then it was time. The man who ushered them in came and told them they had to leave. Nwanyimma saw her raise his hand. It seemed as if he wanted to give her something. She went back. She stretched her hand. Her son squeezed something onto her palm. She closed it.

Out of the building, she opened her palm. It was a rap of Indian hemp. 'What does he want me to do with it? Tell me, what does he want me to do with it?' Nwanyimma said bewildered. Her husband held her.

When they reached home the next day, she sat in their room. The whole place looked strange to her. She turned and asked her husband again: 'Tell me what did he want me to do with it?'

46

# The Child Thief

The traffic was thick as usual on Saturday mornings in Lagos. Bisi was returning from work. She had left the office early, so that she could do some shopping. Her offical hours of duty were such that she did not have much time to shop.

She hesitated for a second with her trafficator pointing to where she wanted to turn to, and the taxi behind her hooting in such a way that if it were a year or so ago, she would have lost control of the steering. But she had known the taxi drivers of Lagos, and how discourteous they were to women drivers. She stopped the car completely, and the trafficator pointed to the other direction. By this time, it was not only the taxi driver who was behind her that hooted, but all the other motorists. 'Go and get a driver,' one shouted. It was not a taxi driver. It was a Lagos motorist.

Bisi smiled and drove slowly and carefully to the car park. She paid, got the piece of paper and waited to cross the Marina to Kingsway Stores. There was no car in view, so she crossed. She hadn't reached the other end, when she saw a familiar face. She crossed quickly and walked up to the lady.

Bisi always did this. The rebuffs she suffered in London, in the hands of schoolmates did not prevent her from enthusiastically greeting anybody she knew back home.

'Agnes,' Bisi called. The lady turned round. Bisi was afraid she might not be Agnes. She had made that mistake before and the lady in question took it very badly. Bisi did not see why anybody should be fussy about a genuine mistake of this nature. She had been mistaken several times for someone else, but she did not take it badly.

47

Agnes turned round. Bisi was about to apologise, when she saw that it was indeed her classmate of ten years ago. 'Bisi,' Agnes called and embraced her. 'How nice to see you. Where have you been all these years?' 'I came back from England three years ago, and you, my, you have grown so fat.' 'And you, you have not changed at all. You still retain that beautiful figure of yours.' 'Come let's go upstairs and find something to eat, coffee or something. Since I came to Lagos, you are the only classmate I have met. I don't know what has happened to the others.'

They went upstairs. Bisi forgot her shopping. It didn't seem as if Agnes had much shopping to do. Kingsway was like *Nkwo* market at home. Whether you have money or not, you went there. Bisi remembered when she was in school in Lagos. She and her friend Ethel used to go to Kingsway every Saturday with six pence each. They went round all the sections, then on their way home, each bought sixpence ice cream.

In the coffee bar, there were many people. Being Saturday, most of them were white women with their children. Their husbands were at work. Bisi ordered coffee for Agnes and some cakes. She ordered coffee for herself and no cakes. 'I am determined to keep my figure,' she said to Agnes. Agnes smiled. It was a sad smile. Bisi noticed it at once, and stopped talking about figures. It just occurred to her then that she should not talk about it for Agnes was so fat. She was a thin girl at school. But that was ten years ago. Ten years is not a short time.

The orders came. Agnes noticed that Bisi did not take sugar. 'No wonder you are so thin. It suits you too. I envy you. I don't care about what I look like these days,' Agnes said. Bisi said nothing.

Bisi knew that there was something that prevented Agnes from being herself. She was sad. She used to be so gay at school, and had a lot of boy friends whom she sacked at will.. She was never short of boy friends.

'When did you come to live in Lagos?' Agnes asked. 'Two

years ago. I worked at Benin for a little while, and decided to come to Lagos. At first I did not like it. But now, I don't think I can work anywhere else.' 'We came to Lagos three years ago. We were in Zaria. You know I was engaged in my final year at school. As soon as I took my School Certificate, I got married, and we went to Zaria. Three years ago we came here. I have not liked it here at all. I'll like to go back to Zaria or somewhere else, not here.' 'But it is so nice here,' Bisi said. 'And now that I know you are here, I'll be paying you visits, and you, you must come and see me. I live at Ikoyi, in a flat with my sister. Come any time you like. Or better still, if you tell me where you live, I shall come and collect you. Has your husband a car?' Before Bisi finished, she was already aware of the tactlessness of the question. Agnes smiled. Her husband had a car, but since they arrived Lagos, she had never been inside it. It was different at Zaria. Her husband took her to places when they were in Zaria. But now, he scarcely remembered that she was there.

'You are not married then,' Agnes asked. Bisi shook her head. 'Not yet,' she said smiling. 'Let's have more coffee.' 'Yes,' Agnes said. Bisi went to the desk to order more cups of coffee. Agnes watched her as she went. She envied her. She was still not married, as beautiful as she was. Don't men see her? Doesn't she appeal to them?

She came back. 'I am delighted to see you today,' Agnes said. 'You don't know it, but this is the only time for a long time that I have actually relaxed. My husband goes to work early and comes home late. By the time he finishes eating, and is ready to go out again, I am already sleepy.'

'And ready to go out again? Don't you go out with him?' Bisi asked. 'Out with him? With my husband? Of course I don't. What for?' 'Oh, you are one of those domesticated females whose place is in the home, mending socks and looking after the children.'

'I have no child, Bisi.'

'You have no child?' Bisi asked in a whisper. Agnes shook her head. 'I have gone everywhere. I cannot recount how

49

many "D and C's" I have had, how many operations. I have never been pregnant, not to talk of abortion. It is my luck. My mother had seven children. Her own mother had nine. I don't see how I should not have even one. Let me be pregnant, and let it be noised that I am pregnant. I don't mind miscarrying it afterwards.'

'Have you tried Dr. . . . . ?' Agnes smiled sadly. 'I have tried him. I tell you, I have gone everywhere. My mother came the other day and said we should go to a native doctor, a few miles away from Lagos. I don't want to go.'

'Why? You should go if your mother suggested it.'

'I am tired of going places. I don't want to go anywhere any more. I have a feeling that one day, they would give me something that will kill me.'

'No, don't say that.'

'Well, that's how I feel at times.'

'What does your husband think about it?' Bisi asked.

'He was sympathetic before, but now he is indifferent, and I don't blame him.'

'Are you sure it is not his fault?'

Agnes began to laugh. Her old gaiety came back to her at that moment. When she finished laughing, she said. 'It is not Mike's fault. He has two boys. They are in Zaria.'

'They are his children?'

'Of course. You see them and know that they are my husband's children.' She lifted the cup of coffee. It was cold now. Bisi watched her. Her hand shook as she drank the last drop.

'You are God sent,' Agnes said to Bisi. 'Lagos is a strange place. There are lots of people, yet you can't talk to any of them. I don't know whether people at home know how lonely one can be in Lagos. There is nobody I can talk to here, as I am talking to you. You see.'

They did some shopping together. It was obvious that neither had any serious shopping to do. Agnes asked Bisi to take her home, so she would know where they lived. Bisi readily agreed. She did not mind the traffic. 'I don't think I'll

50

ever drive in Lagos,' Agnes said.

'Before I came to work in Lagos, I said so. When I came I just started driving, just as I drove in Benin, and now, I am used to it. It requires guts though.'

Bisi drove on in silence. She remembered Agnes, and how lively she used to be at school, and how cheeky. She had set ideas about marriage. She had said that she was not going to marry anybody who had no car. She dreamt of evenings out when her husband returned from work, and how he would open the car for her to enter, and all that. She was going to dress very well to please her husband. She was not going to be like other girls who refused to look good after the first baby had arrived. She was of course not going to breastfeed the baby, for it was messy. All she was going to do, was take some tablets and the breast milk would dry up. She was going to have four children, two boys and two girls. She was going to have a wonderful home. She was not going to work. Looking after her husband and children were enough to occupy her. She was so sophisticated.

And now, here was Agnes, ten years after, with a husband who no longer cares, and no children. It was only when she spoke that one knew that she went to school. She had sadly neglected herself. She was not beautiful, but she was pretty, full of pranks, and had the zest to live. Someone else was sharing her husband with her, and there was nothing she could do about it.

'I saw Helen the other day. She did not recognise me,' Agnes began.

'Which Helen?'

'Onobanjo.' Bisi laughed. 'When we were at school,' Bisi said, 'and you went on holiday, if Helen saw you, she did not recognise you, let alone now. How did you expect her to greet you?' 'She was with a tall white man. Is she married to a white man?' 'I don't know. I won't be surprised if she married a white man. She behaved strangely at school. She had that air about her which we ridiculed. Our ridicule did not change her. It rather made her more determined to behave strangely.'

'Turn right now,' Agnes directed.

'Right?'

'Yes, right.'

'I have some relations here you know. That house over there. I must see them on my way back.' 'It's a one way street.' 'Yes. Let me stop now. You are not in a hurry?' 'Oh no. It is kind of you. If I had taken a bus, it would take me hours to get home.' Bisi wondered when last she took a bus. It was in London. The day she left London, in fact, she had taken a bus to Victoria Station where the BOAC bus conveyed them to the airport. It would be fun to take a bus once again.

She stopped the car, and Agnes preferred to remain while she went in. Her cousin and the husband were in. The children were all in. So she went back to the car to call Agnes. Agnes reluctantly went in, and sat down on the only chair in the room. Bisi sat on the bed. They wanted to buy them beer, but Bisi protested and said she wanted just kola. They brought kola and her cousin's husband broke the kola and they ate.

'Nobody sees you these days,' her cousin said. She was a year older. She had only three years of formal education. But they were still friends and when they saw each other, they always had a lot to talk about.

'You live down the road?' Bisi's cousin said to Agnes.

'Yes, down the road,' Agnes said.

'Do you know her?' Bisi asked.

'I have seen her many times,' Bisi's cousin said. She did not want to say more. 'We were together at school. And this afternoon, we met at the Kingsway Stores for the first time in ten years. Isn't that wonderful? She has grown huge for nothing,' Bisi said with mischief in her eyes. 'I am much older than she is.'

'Don't mind her,' Agnes said laughing.

'Bisi, what is good about you is that you look younger and

52

younger every day,' her cousin said. One of her children ran in. 'Aunty Bisi,' she said, 'you promised to take me home with you last week.' 'All right. Go and wear your clean dress. I am taking you home with me today. But we must agree on one thing. You are not going to cry. If you cry for your mother, I shall spank you.' The child thought for a little while. They watched her. She shook her head and ran out of the room. She had been to Bisi before to stay for a weekend. Bisi went to take her on a Friday afternoon. Before eight o'clock, she was such a nuisance, that Bisi had to bring her back before her parents went to bed.

Agnes watched the little girl, and Bisi watched Agnes. She understood and got up. 'We are going. Come and see me next weekend. Or better still, I shall come and collect you. Agnes, let's go.' Agnes thanked them for the kola and they were about to drive off, when Agnes asked her to stop. Just then a little boy of about five came up to the car. Agnes looked at him intently. 'Bisi,' she whispered, 'this is one of my husband's children. What is he doing here?'

'Your husband's child?'

'Yes. So Amina is in Lagos. No wonder I don't see Mike these days. He doesn't even eat when he returns home. So she has come to Lagos.' At that time, Bisi's cousin came out. 'Did you forget anything?' she asked.

'No,' Bisi said and started the car.

'Wait. Let me find out whether his mother is here,' Agnes said. Bisi beckoned to her cousin and when she came, they asked her whether the boy's mother was living nearby.

'She lives in that house,' Bisi's cousin said pointing to a storey building a few houses away.

'Do you know her?' she asked.

'Agnes knows her. Let's go then,' Bisi said quickly as she saw Agnes' face. She was almost in tears.

When they arrived at Agnes' house, there was nobody in. She told Bisi that her husband was working night shift that week. She gave the servant off that day, thinking she would return in the evening. The house was not a bad one by any standard, but it was obvious that Agnes had not bothered to do anything to it. The cushion covers were old and worn out, and besides, very dirty. Bisi could not forgive Agnes for that one at least. She could understand the cushion covers being old, but not dirty. Surely the servant could be asked to wash them.

She brought Bisi some soft drink. The glass was not properly washed, and Bisi could not bear that. 'What is the matter Agnes?'

'About what?'

'The glass. It is dirty.'

'Oh yes, it is. I am confused, Bisi. I am sorry. Let me bring a clean one. So Amina is in Lagos. She refused to come to Lagos.' Bisi said nothing. She knew that Agnes was not talking to her in particular. She was just thinking aloud.

She came back with a clean glass, and poured out the soft drink. Bisi drank it all in one gulp. 'I don't sip soft drinks when I am thirsty,' she said.

'You know. . .' Agnes said. It did not seem as if she heard what Bisi said about sipping soft drinks. 'You know, my husband spent so much on the children. He begged Amina to give him the children, that I would look after them, but she refused. I sent people to plead with her. She refused. Now she is in Lagos. Perhaps she was not getting on well in Zaria anymore. And what baffles me is that my husband has not mentioned it. Well, that would depend on when she arrived. I shall ask him tonight when he returns.'

'Yes, ask him,' Bisi echoed. She didn't know what to say.

'Amina cost my husband so much money and she has come to Lagos.'

'Do you think she would like to come here and live with you and your husband?' Bisi asked. Agnes laughed, before she replied.

'No. She will not. You don't know Amina. Even in Zaria she refused to come and live with us.'

'You mean that you would have allowed her to come to your matrimonial home to live with your husband?'

'Of course. What else could I do? By coming to stay with us, my husband would be in, and I would have a chance, if nothing else, to feel his presence. I wouldn't have minded at all. The mother of my husband's children? When I have none of my own?'

Marriage must be strange. That was what Bisi thought of it as she drove home. It did not make any meaning to her. What did it all mean, if Agnes, after ten years of it was in that state of mind. But Agnes' case was different. If she had a child, it would have been much better. She would not have been in such a strain. And she was helpless. What was she to do? What could she do for Agnes? She knew that she was prepared to do anything for her. She wanted her to be happy. But she could not be happy unless she had a child. For her that was the only source of happiness. She believed that her husband would treat her better if she had a child for him. She knew that Amina refused to give up the children because she realised that if she did, she would have no hold on him anymore. She was not a fool. She knew what she wanted.

Bisi was surprised one day to see Agnes in her office. She was sadder than the day they met which was about a month ago. Her eyes were a bit swollen from crying. She asked her to sit down and asked the messenger to make coffee for her.

When the coffee was made, Agnes almost took it greedily. She said she needed it. She had not eaten anything for days.

'Tell me what has happened,' she asked Agnes.

'My husband has given me the sack. His people arrived the other day and after consulting with them, they told me to pack and leave. Since Amina was coming to stay, and since I could not bear to stay with her, which was a lie, and since I have no child, I am the one to leave for her.'

'Were all these said or implied?'

'They were said. What did it matter if they were merely implied? It had the same effect on me.'

'So what are you going to do?' Bisi was afraid when she asked this question. She was afraid because she thought that Agnes would ask her for accommodation. She was thinking of the lie to tell. Already she remembered telling her that her sister was staying with her in the flat. She would add that her mother was coming next week with a friend.

'I can't go home,' Agnes said. Bisi was becoming more and more worried. That's the penalty of being too friendly. That's why in London, Nigerian students ran away from one another, for fear of being encroached upon.

'No, you can't go home. But you want to stay in Lagos?'

'Yes. I have a small business. I sew and and sell some foodstuff, and they bring in quite some money. I am looking for a place to stay. I'll like to stay either in Yaba or Ebute-Metta. A lot of girls I make dresses for are there.'

'So you sew,' Bisi said wondering the type of girls Agnes made dresses for. One look at her would make a prospective customer change her mind about taking materials to her to sew. 'I'll make inquiries for you,' Bisi said casually. She felt better now. 'How are you generally?' she asked.

'I cannot be worse than I am right now. Oh, my mother is coming. I have asked her to come and stay a little while with me. You have a beautiful office,' Agnes said.

'Well, it is not bad.'

A messenger came into the room and told Bisi that her boss wanted to see her. Agnes got up quickly and said she was going. 'Sit down. I'll take you back,' she said. She sat down.

When they were driving to Agnes' she was a bit relaxed. She told Bisi that each time she saw her, she felt better.

'And do you know why you feel like that?' Bisi asked.

'No,' Agnes replied.

'You feel better because I am older than you are. We were classmates, and although you had been married for ten years, I am not married, so in a way you are slightly better than I am.'

'Oh no,' Agnes shouted. But she knew that it was the truth. She had not put her thoughts in words, and it sounded so horrible now that Bisi had put them in words for her.

'So in spite of your misfortunes, you feel better in my company.'

'Oh please don't say that. Please.'

After work, Bisi went to see her cousin. She told her about Agnes. Her cousin was sorry. 'I know that woman,' she said to Bisi, 'the mother of those lovely boys. She is so lazy she can hardly take a broom and sweep the house. You hear her shouting at the maid. The maid goes to the market, cooks the food, washes the children and their clothes. She does absolutely nothing. She doesn't know whether her children eat or not. And they are never ill. God has a way of doing these things. Look at the care I take of my children, yet there is hardly any month I don't go to the hospital for one ailment or the other. She is lucky. So the man is going to take her into his house. Good for her.'

'You know of a house Agnes could move to?' Bisi asked.

'She asked you to look for accommodation for her?'

'Yes. Why do you ask in that way?'

'She has been here long. She knows people in this area. You came to Lagos only last year.'

'I have been here for two years,' Bisi said.

'Well, we shall see. I shall make inquiries.'

In a fortnight, Bisi was able to get a place for Agnes. She moved in with all her things, and sent for her mother. She moved out with a minimum amount of fuss. It seemed as if she had given up fighting for her husband. A year or two ago, she would have raised hell. Now it did not matter. She still loved her husband, but what could she do if her husband did not love her any more?

When her mother arrived, she brought her so many things from home, and she was happy that her mother still treated her like a child. What worried her in this visit was her mother's questions. She was going to ask all sorts of questions, and make all sorts of suggestions. She was thankful that her mother did not begin to ask questions about her husband. Each time Agnes' mother came, she was always on Agnes' side when her husband molested her. She

57

was not surprised that now they were separated.

After a week, Agnes' mother told her that she brought a native doctor with her, and that he was staying at Ajegunle. The native doctor had come to give her treatment and she was hopeful that something good would come out of it. So in the evening, they took a bus and went to Ajegunle. Agnes was examined. The native doctor gave her some medicine, but asked her to get some mercury which he was going to use for medicine for her.

Apart from hearing about mercury at school, Agnes had not heard of mercury again. She did not do science at school, so she did not even know what it looked like. It surprised her that it could be used as medicine.

The only person she could go to was Bisi. So in the morning, she went to Bisi's office. Bisi saw that she looked much better. She was relaxed, and she had made efforts to look clean. The dress did not fit, but it did not matter. It is better to have a clean dress. She also plaited her hair, so that it was tidier than what Bisi was used to.

'You look gorgeous,' Bisi said.

'Thank you,' Agnes said and felt gorgeous. She told Bisi her mission, and she promised to get it for her. Agnes opened her bag and brought out some groundnuts and fruits she bought for Bisi. Bisi thanked her.

A week did not pass when Agnes came again. 'This is not the right one,' she said. She was near tears. 'The man said that it is the red one.'

'Mercury oxide,' Bisi said.

'Do you think you can get it?' Agnes asked.

'I'll try.'

'Thank you. God will reward you. You are God sent.'

When Agnes left, Bisi went to the man who gave her the mercury. The man was beginning to be curious. He asked questions and paid attention to the answers. Bisi told him about Agnes. He did not know her, so it did not matter at all, and of course Bisi did not want to be suspected in that way. But he was her colleague and he had a right to know what she wanted to do with it.

'I have been wondering myself,' her colleague said. 'You know what? Someone came to me about a month ago and asked me to give him some mercury. You know we are the only people, I mean people of our profession, who are entitled to possess mercury in the labs. So I asked him what he wanted to do with it. He smiled. He did not answer. He put his hand into his pocket. I watched him, and he brought out a bundle of notes. I stared at him. "Have it and you will be in partnership with me. You can easily get it, and I can't, you see." I was dazed. At first I didn't realise what he meant. Then slowly I understood. The man was buying me with his money. So I said, "If you don't leave my house this minute, I shall call in the police." He got up, shook his head, took a step, turned and said, "You don't want to be rich eh? Does money sting you? Go and sit down. University people like you make money in all sorts of ways. You'll call the police . . ." and he laughed. The way he laughed was what exasperated me, not so much what he said. So you see why I was curious about your demand. I wondered what they were doing with it. However, I shall give you a little for your friend. I quite sympathise with her.'

Bisi did not see Agnes again for nearly six months. She had gone home on leave, and when she came back, she travelled to Ghana. It was when she was returning from work one day that she saw Agnes along the Marina. She parked her car in one of the car parks and embraced her. 'I can't believe it,' Bisi said.

'I can't believe it myself,' Agnes said.

'And how is he?'

'When he heard, he came and collected me.'

'He came and collected you?'

'Yes, he came and collected me.'

'And you went?' Bisi asked.

'Why not. The child is his. He is my husband.'

'And Amina?'

'She has gone, taking the two boys with her. She is using

them as a bait. I am sorry for the children.'

'Congratulations,' Bisi said.

'Don't congratulate me now. Wait until the baby arrives. Then congratulate me then. I am so scared. I have waited for the past ten years. I can't believe it. I am afraid of talking about it.'

'Oh don't worry. It will be all right. When is it due?'

'March or so, I don't really know exactly.'

March came and Agnes did not have the baby. Her husband was getting anxious. As for Agnes she was losing weight. She was not sure whether the baby was kicking or not. One day, she told her husband she wanted to go home. He did not want her to go home, not in her state. But she insisted until he let her go. By then, she was ten months pregnant, and she was beginning to feel that something was really wrong, only she did not tell her husband.

Her mother did not want her to see a medical doctor in the hospital nearby. She rather preferred the native doctors. After all wasn't it the native doctor who treated her before she was pregnant?

Nothing happened for another month. So one day when her mother was not in, she went to the hospital. A doctor examined her, found her case interesting and asked her to come the next day.

After the examination, Agnes was told that she was not pregnant. It did not quite come as a surprise. She felt it all along. True, she did not menstruate all these months, and she felt movements in her womb. Yet she knew that all was not well. the doctor told her that if she wanted, he would operate on her and get out the tumour.

Agnes locked up herself in her room. She wept. She did not want to tell her mother. Her mother will not believe it. What was she going to do? So she wasn't going to have a baby? Meanwhile, a letter came from her husband, asking how she felt. He tried as much as possible to conceal his anxiety.

Agnes knew that she had to do something before her

60

husband became suspicious. Already people were talking as they were wont to talk. That night, she did not sleep. She remembered Bisi and wondered whether she should write to her. There was no point. She would tell her everything when she went back to Lagos.

Then an idea struck her. She was horrified that she should think in that direction. Yet, the idea gripped her, and she could not shake it off. The idea was not entirely new. She remembered that a prophet in Lagos had asked her to do it. All she needed to do was get a newly born baby, nurse it for a month or two, then hand it over to its mother. But how was that possible. Where would she get a baby? She had no relatives who were having children. But what mother would willingly give her baby for that purpose? The prophets of Lagos were a queer lot.

She and her mother were outside the house one evening when someone came. She sat down and kola was brought to her. Conversation followed conversation, and the woman told them about a woman who was two years pregnant. She had the baby all right, but she died in the process and the child lived. 'God forbid. Any child that is coming to the world only to kill its mother, should be far from my daughter,' Agnes' mother said. The story was horrifying, but strangely enough, it gave Agnes hopes. Two whole years. If what the woman said was true, then she was not all that bad off. She had only done twelve months.

Agnes went to the hospital. She saw the doctor again. She told him she was ready for the operation. The doctor had a clinic a few miles away from the hospital. The operation would be done there.

She told her mother she was going to have the baby in the hospital. She wondered whether she was going to ask someone to carry out her plan for her, or carry it out herself. She couldn't do it herself. She arranged for a taxi driver to help her get away.

Her mother prepared everything for the baby. She got her a maid who came to the house to get used to it before the

61

baby arrived. She was already getting fond of Agnes. Agnes had promised that she would take her to Lagos, and she was pleased about it. The day before Agnes left for the hospital, her mother received a message summoning her to Aba. Agnes was happy at the turn of events. She did not tell her mother exactly what she was going to do in the hospital, and now, she was called away, as if she planned it. She must not fail. Now that her husband wanted and needed her, she should not disappoint him. She must take a baby to him at all costs.

The operation was not complicated. In a few days, she was all right, and the doctor discharged her.

The taxi driver was waiting. He hooted to reassure her. Agnes went into the maternity ward and grabbed the first baby she saw. The sex of the baby did not matter. Nobody saw her. As she was walking into the street to get into the taxi, she saw the doctor. He waved to her. He had so many patients. Agnes was only one of them. She got into the taxi and drove off.

The next morning, she left for Lagos with the baby and the maid. It was Bisi that she first saw in the house, then her husband and a few friends. They all got up and welcomed her. Bisi grabbed the baby. 'A baby boy. Welcome, welcome baby,' Bisi said.

'He is exactly like Mike,' one friend said.

'Yes, just like Mike, but he has Agnes' nose.'

The baby began to cry, and they handed it over to Agnes. 'I came to check whether you were back or not. I hadn't stayed thirty minutes when you came back. Congrats. Now I can congratulate you in full. I told you the baby will come out all right. Eh, so I said,' Bisi said holding the baby's thumb.

Mike was very happy. He bought drinks and his friends drank. They made merry. 'There is hope for every woman,' someone said. Agnes heard it. She nearly swooned. 'I'll like to lie down,' she said to her husband. 'I am very tired.'

'Come over here. You shouldn't have travelled so quickly.

I said I was coming to fetch you. Why didn't you wait for me? Didn't you get my letter?'

'I did. The expense, your job, and all that. I decided to come home. Mother will come later. Please call Bisi for me.'

'I'll see you some other time. I am tired now. I have something important to say to you,' she said to Bisi.

'Of course. I am going away right now. I shall see you later here.' And Bisi squeezed a pound note on the palm of the baby and closed the delicate palm.

* * *

When they came, the C.I.D., they knocked at the door. The maid was there. She was washing the napkins used the night before. Agnes was still sleeping. She was surprised at her own peace within herself. She knew that what she did was criminal, but it didn't seem to bother her. She expected the C.I.D., only not so soon. Why should they come now and deprive her of her joy? The baby wasn't hers, but what did it matter? For nearly a week, she lived in a make believe world which she had no wish to terminate so soon.

The maid came in and told her that two men were outside. 'Ask them to come in,' she said. The two men came into the bedroom and greeted her. 'The baby is sleeping. Please don't wake him up.' She called the maid and whispered something into her ears. Then she asked the two men to go and sit down in the sitting room. She would have her bath quickly and be with them.

The two men did as they were told. Agnes controlled the whole thing. She was soon dressed, and came out. The men declined the beer offered them. They told the maid it was too early to drink beer.

'You have come to find out about my baby,' she said to them.

'Yes,' one replied.

'You are married, and you, you are married too.'

'Yes,' the two men were compelled to answer.

63

'And your wives have children.'

'Yes,' the two men replied.

'Well, I have been married for over ten years. This is my first baby. If you want to take it, you have to take me as well.'

'We'll take both of you.'

'And the maid? You have to take her as well so that she can feed the baby. I am tired.'

'Don't worry. We'll take care of the baby.'

She called the maid. When she came she asked her to bring out the baby's things. She brought them out. 'You see, I made provision for the baby. I am not just an ordinary child thief. I wanted to have him as mine, not to sell him.'

'You should have adopted one.'

'I didn't want to adopt a baby. I wanted to have a baby. Take me. I am going like this with you.'

When they came out, Agnes was surprised to see that lots of people were outside. The usual Lagos crowd. They did not throw stones at her. They did not shout. They folded their hands on their chests and watched Agnes being taken into the car. How did they know?

They drove away, and women were talking in whispers. Mike drove in. He saw the car on the way, the car that carried Agnes and 'his baby' to the police station. He turned and followed them in his car.

# The Delinquent Adults

Ozoemena's mother came in and sat down on the bed. She sat up when she saw her mother enter the room. The room was dark and there was no air coming in through the small window which was high. Wire gauze was used to further block the little air that managed to come in. If all had been well for Ozoemena, she would have torn off the wire gauze, or refused to stay in the room. But all was not well with her.

'Have you eaten?' her mother asked her. She shook her head.

'Why have you not eaten?'

'I am not hungry,' she said.

'Did you eat yesterday?'

'No.'

'You did not eat yesterday. You did not eat day before, and today, you have not eaten. You want to die of hunger?'

'I am not hungry.'

'I know you won't be hungry, but you must make yourself, force yourself to eat something. This is not the end of the world for you. The day is just breaking for you. You hear, my daughter. Get up and eat something. I have brought some food for you.'

Ozoemena began to cry. She remembered the whole incident. In the night before the incident she had dreamt a bad dream. She and her husband were travelling, to where she did not know. Her two boys were with them. She dressed them beautifully. She too dressed herself well. Her husband was gorgeously dressed though he did not care about clothes. He often told her that he lived for her and the two children. Once they were properly clothed and well fed, he was all right.

They came to an open place where cattle were grazing. The grass was green and very fresh, and there was a man who was standing by. He was not minding the cattle, he was just standing there. Ozoemena recognised him at once and called him by his name. 'Ewoo, the daughter of Ogbenyan, what are you doing here? Eh, what are you doing here?' Ozoemena could not answer. 'You must be mad,' the man went on. 'You must be off your head to come so far.' It was then that Ozoemena replied and said she was with her husband. 'With your husband? Well, your husband being here is understandable. But why should he bring you along too? why should you bring her along and your two boys?' the man said to Ozoemena's husband. He said nothing to him. He was on the move all the time. He did not look up. He neither turned to the right, nor to the left. 'His own is finished,' the man said to Ozoemena. 'It is finished. It was finished long ago. His ancestors have taken him. Don't you see how steadfastly he is walking so as to cross the river before the ferryman goes home? So you must come back. Go home my sister, take your children home. They are such fine children. Please take them home.'

Ozeoemena went on as she saw her husband in front without minding what the man was saying. 'You foolish girl,' the man said. 'You headstrong girl,' he said again. And as he said this, he snatched the two boys from her grip and ran.

Ozoemena did not mind this. She walked on behind her husband until they came to the river. The ferryman was there.

'Good. I am happy I am not late,' her husband said.
'Late for what?' Ozoemena asked.
'For crossing the river.'
'You are crossing the river?' Ozoemena asked in horror.
'Yes. Didn't you know?'
'You are crossing that river?' Ozoemena asked again. But

66

her husband did not say a word. He merely brushed her aside and entered the canoe. Ozoemena wanted to enter, but he pushed her away and shouted at the ferryman to push off.

Ozoemena put her hands on her head and began to cry. She beckoned to her husband to come back, but he did not hear her. As she was crying, the man who snatched her children appeared from nowhere. This time he had changed his clothes, and had a walking stick in his hand. 'Has he gone?' he ask Ozoemena.

'So you knew he was going?'

'Of course I knew. That was why I did not want you to go with him.'

'And you allowed him to go?'

'And you, could you stop him from going?'

'No.'

'Well then.'

'Won't he come back?'

'No.'

'Why?'

'The journey takes years.'

'What journey?'

'You are asking like a child.'

'I am not a child.' Ozoemena did not want to be called a child. She was a mother of two children. But she was not quite twenty years old.

'Let's go home. I shall take you home. Don't worry. You can do nothing about it,' the man said and took Ozoemena home. When they reached home, she heard one of her children crying. She got up. Her husband was sleeping beside her. Her son had left his bed and had come to his parents' bed. They lived in a room and a parlour.

She carried her son, and put him on her stomach and lured him to sleep again. Then she placed her hand on her husband's chest. His heart was beating. She did it again, and it was beating normally. 'Thank God,' she said.

'What are you thanking God for?' her husband asked in his characteristic way.

67

'Oh, you are awake. It is nothing. I dreamt Chukwuemeka fell from the bed. I woke up and saw him beside the bed.'

'Did he climb out from the bed by himself?' he asked.

'Yes,' the boy replied.

'Oh, he is awake. I thought he was sleeping. What time is it?'

'It must be six o'clock.'

Ozoemena's husband got up, and sat on the bed. He took the child from his wife, and hugged him. 'Each morning, you wake us up. What makes you wake up so early when your younger brother is asleep?' The child went on crying, saying he was hungry. 'This early in the morning? Ozoemena, take your child and give him food. I must get ready for work. I don't want the Chief Clerk, the wicked Chief Clerk to talk to me harshly.'

'Hasn't he changed?' Ozoemena asked.

'Changed from what to what? How can he change? He lords it over everybody in the office. He is not pleased with anything you do. And he is so officious, so very officious. He makes me laugh at times. But there are times he is jovial, like the day he told us about the fight between himself and his wife. His wife was headstrong. She was huge and quarrelsome, but he did not want to beat her. She had been so good to him, and she had borne him fine children. But that day in particular, she shamed him in the presence of his friends, and so he beat her black and blue. In spite of her bulk, he felled her, and with a cane, thrashed her so much that she cried out for mercy. We all laughed, not because we did not feel for the poor woman, but because of the way he told the story. Ozoemena, I must get ready for work. Let me have my bath quickly.'

Ozoemena's husband had his bath. By the time he was ready, breakfast was ready. It consisted of akara balls and corn flour. Ozoemena could not take flour without sugar, but her husband was sick if he swallowed a spoonful of corn flour in which sugar had been added. He ate quickly and mounted his bicycle and went to work.

68

Ozoemena remembered that day. She was to go to the market, and buy food that will last them about four days. But she found it difficult that morning to be up and doing. She slowly had her bath and asked the maid to bathe her children and give them breakfast. She did this herself, but she did not feel like it that morning. She took great care of her children.

Then she went to a friend next door and told her all about her dream in the night. 'Do you believe in dreams?' her friend asked her.

'Yes and no,' Ozoemena replied. 'You see at school, I was a great dreamer. The girls called me Joseph. My dreams at school were like fairy tales. There were three of us who vied for the first place in our class. Before or after the exam, I would dream a dream. The three of us climbed a hill. If I was the first to reach the top, I was sure to be first that term, if second, I was the second and so on.'

'So you think that the dream you dreamt is a bad one?' her friend asked.

'I don't know what I think. I know I don't like it, and that I am not myself this morning. I feel hollow.'

'Did you tell him?'

'No, I didn't. I was afraid.'

'And he has gone to work?'

'Yes, he has gone to work.'

'Don't worry. Go to the market. Nothing will happen to him. Just go your own way. Don't quarrel with anybody in the market.'

Ozoemena thanked her friend and went home. She was the shadow of herself in the market. When she returned, she cooked and gave her children food to eat. She looked at the time. It was past the time that her husband should return. Fear gripped her. She waited. She rearranged the table again. She opened the two dishes to make sure everything was all right. Then for want of any useful thing to do, she went into the bedroom and changed her dress, and put finishing touches to make-up. She was a beautiful woman.

69

She ran out as she heard her name. 'Is Ozoemena in, is she in. Come out, we are lost, we are dead. Come out quickly.'

It was her sister-in-law. 'Our brother has betrayed us. Chukwuma has betrayed us. What are we going to do? Ozoemena, what are you going to do? And your children? *Ewoo* daylight has suddenly turned into darkness for us.'

Ozoemena fainted.

Ozoemena's husband was returning from work when he was crushed by a lorry. It was not his fault. The lorry had no brakes. A few relatives who lived in Port Harcourt came together and with their help, the body was conveyed home where they buried him. Ozoemena could not forget the journey with the corpse from Port Harcourt to their home. It was done at night. Palm fronds were put in front of the lorry to warn people that a corpse was in the lorry. The driver drove very slowly. He stopped many times, and Ozoemena who was in front with him wondered why he made all those stops.

They reached home at last, and the next day he was buried. It was a week after the burial that Ozoemena's mother came determined that her daughter was going to eat something, for she had refused to eat anything since the death of her husband.

'Wipe your tears my daughter and get up and eat. You will die of hunger. You have cried enough for your husband. You must eat.' After much persuasion, Ozoemena got up, and washed her hands and began to eat.

'Has your husband's brother seen you yet?'

'No.'

'Do you know why he wants to see you?'

'No,' Ozoemena said. She did not want to discuss that just then.

'And your husband's property? Was everything brought down from Port Harcourt?'

'Everything was brought down. There was nothing left.'

'Did you check?'

'Yes, I checked.'

'I know why I am asking. Your husband's people would like to know everything. They would think you are hiding some property from them.'

'They would think so?' Ozoemena asked, horrified.

'Yes, didn't you know?'

'No, I didn't know. Why must they do that?'

'Well, I don't know. But I am speaking from experience, my daughter. When my husband died, his people molested me. His brother especially molested me. You see we were not friends, and according to our custom he was to marry me. And I resented this. I did not like him. Our people said I was a bad woman, but I did not heed them. I knew what I wanted. I knew I did not want to marry him. It caused so much trouble, and the fact that I did not have a son contributed to their making things so difficult for me. I had to leave your father's house. That's why I am particular, my daughter. But you are all right. You have two sons. They will always remember that, so they won't treat you badly. But tell me, is it true that your husband has several bags of money in the bank?'

Ozoemena opened her mouth and closed it again. She shook her head and adjusted herself properly. There was a knock at the door. 'Who is that? Come in, come right in.' Ozoemena's mother opened the door. 'It is you. Sit down here. You have come to see your sister. Please help me talk to her. I am her mother. I have had the experience. I don't have to tell you this, you know. Beg her for me to eat. To eat just a little.'

'Ozoemena, are you still crying? I have told you not to cry any more. Think of your children. Think of all of us. Listen to me. Wipe your tears,' Ozoemena's sister-in-law said to her. This brought even more tears to Ozoemena's eyes. She fought very hard to suppress the tears.

'You brought her food,' her sister-in-law said to her mother.

'Yes, I brought her food,' but she won't eat.'

'Don't worry, I shall eat. When I feel hungry, I shall eat.'

71

The two women looked at each other and shrugged their shoulders.

'How are your children?' Ozoemena's mother asked her sister-in-law.

'They are well.'

'One of them had yaws. Is he well now?'

'Oh yes, he is well now. I now know that yaws is very contagious.'

'I told you. How did you discover it?'

'Immediately one of my sons had it, I sent him to the farm to go and live with my sister. I made sure of course that I brought back my sister's children from the farm to stay with me. So my sister treated the yaws, and when it healed, my son came back. And now none of my children has it. I know of families where all the children have yaws at the same time.'

'I told you. It was one white woman who visited our church sometime ago who told us. Ozoemena was in the boarding school then. I think it was her first year at the boarding school. She told the church woman, when she was talking about health generally, that yaws was contagious, and that we must isolate our children when they suffer from it. I am glad your son is well now and that your other children were not affected. When was this? It is a long time you know.'

'It is a long time indeed. It must be about six months ago.'

'That was before your visit to us in Port Harcourt,' Ozoemena said.

'Yes it was before then. My brother was alive then. Death. How you kill? Let me go, Ozoemena, before I start asking our gods and ancestors why they let Chukwuma leave us.'

When she left, Ozoemena's mother continued. 'Yes, I heard that he left several bags of money in the bank. A friend told me, and said she heard it from a reliable source. Are the bags of money in the bank? Can you get the money?'

'Ewoo, mother, why are you talking like that? Why must I think of that now? And why are you talking as if the money means everything to me, as if money will bring back my husband from the land of the dead.'

'You are a child, my daughter. Remember you have children. You must live. You seem to forget that. However, tell me how many bags of money did he leave in the bank?'

'Bags of money?'

'Yes, bags of money.'

'I don't know about bags of money, mother. My husband had some savings. How much that is, I have not bothered to find out.'

'You have not bothered to find out?'

'No.'

'You must find out quickly.'

'Why is it so urgent, mother?'

'You will understand in due course. I had a bad experience when my husband died. I don't want you to suffer, that's all.'

'Am I going to suffer, mother? Do widows always suffer?'

'You won't suffer, my daughter. You are still young. You will marry again.'

'I am not going to marry again.'

'You won't marry again?'

'I am going to look after my husband's children. Marriage is out of the question for me.'

'That is right my daughter. Such fine boys must be properly looked after.'

They heard the voice of Chukwuma's brother. He was the head of the family. He was scolding one of his wives who left her child crying. The wife was trying to explain to him, but he did not want to hear. 'Is Ozoemena at home?' he called. Ozoemena's mother came out, and greeted him. He answered very coldly, so Ozoemena's mother greeted again.

'Adishiemea. I am greeting you, our Uzonwane.'

'Nwadiugwu, I answered you.'

'I didn't know you answered. I didn't hear you.'

'Perhaps you are looking for your ear,' Chukwuma's brother said.

'Perhaps you want me to ask you whether you are looking for your own ear. I know that I hear well. People doubt whether you hear well. You don't want me to say in public what our people think of your hearing faculty.'

'Ntianu, you are prepared for me today.'

'No, you are prepared for me,' Ozoemena's mother said.

'Why are you so quarrelsome?'

'I should ask you. You started the quarrel.'

'You did.'

'I didn't, you did,' Ozoemena's mother said. 'I am prepared for anything. My daughter is in there. If anything happens to her, I shall hold you responsible.'

'What do you think will happen to your daughter? You talk like a child. Who will lay hands on a young widow with two young children? There must be something wrong with you.'

'No, nothing is wrong with me. It is you, you whose head is not correct.'

'Ugwutte, Ntianu, they must have sent you to me today. Tell those who sent you that you did not find me. You hear. Tell them you cannot find me. Two of us cannot talk. Your daughter married my brother, my flesh and blood. Whatever I say to you, I say to myself, and my brother's children. So you. So you see, you are wrong. You are not behaving well. Where is my daughter?' he said and went into the room. They had been talking in the sitting room. And Ozoemena heard all they said to each other.

Uzonwane and Ntianu were not friends. The misunderstanding came when Chukwuma announced that he was going to marry Ozoemena, his brother did all in his power to prevent the marriage. He did not like it. He was suspicious of girls who went to school. He feared that they were too wise, wiser than their ages, and that Ozoemena was going to dominate his brother, and make him not care for his own family. Naturally, neither Ozoemena nor her mother liked this especially as Uzonwane did not hide his objection to the marriage. Ntianu did not forget it in spite of the fact that Chukwuma could not help feeling that Uzonwane was now saying in his mind, 'Serves you right.

74

I told you not to marry her.'

'How are you today?' Uzonwane asked the young widow.

'I am well,' she said.

'Please don't worry. Your mother and I don't see eye to eye in many things.'

'Yes,' she said.

'What about your children?'

'They are well,' she said. She paused for a little while. 'I am anxious about one thing.' she said.

'What, my daughter?'

'About their education. The oldest was going to school before his father died. I would want him to continue,' she said. 'But he is only three years old.'

'Yes. He was going to a special school.'

'A special school?'

'Yes.'

'In Port Harcourt?'

'Yes, in Port Harcourt.'

'And how much did Chukwuma pay for him as school fees?' Ozoemena told him. The man cracked his fingers. No wonder his brother did not think of building a house if he had to spend so much for a child for one term.

'It is well, my daughter. We shall settle that. That is not the main problem. How much did your husband leave in the bank?'

'I don't know.'

'You have not bothered to find out?'

'No.'

'That is strange. It did not occur to you?'

'No,' Ozoemena said. She was surprised. What were these old people up to? Her mother had talked of bags of money, and now her brother-in-law. Next, perhaps her sister-in-law. What was more important? The memory of her husband or the amount of money left in the bank? When she was young, she heard a story which she did not quite understand then. Now it was making some impression on her. A woman was living with her husband in Lagos. Her husband died

75

suddenly, and before her husband's people knew of the man's death, the woman had hidden all the property of her husband. The relatives of her husband had to collect money to buy clothes to cover the dead man's body. Well, so the story went. Ozoemena was a little girl, and she wondered how the story could be true. It was a shock to her, that her brother-in-law and other people could think that the first thing that could occur to her after the sudden death of her husband was to hide his money and property.

The way her brother-in-law asked the questions showed that he did not trust her at all. 'She has said "no" to your questions. Won't you leave her in peace, Uzonwane? Won't you leave my daughter who lost such a husband in peace? She is a little girl you know. She would have been in school if she did not marry your brother.'

'And my brother would not have died if your daughter were in school by now.'

Ozoemena was hysterical. She shouted and shouted, until all the neighbours came round.

'So I killed him,' Ozoemena said to her mother ten times over. 'So that's what they say. That I killed him so that I will look after my children all alone. So that I can live all alone with my children. Mother, is that what they are saying? Tell me, is that what they are saying? Even my sister-in-law?'

Ozoemena's mother said nothing to her. She had nothing to say.

'Why don't you say anything to me, mother? Didn't they know that Chukwuma died accidentally? Who didn't know that?'

'They are not saying that you killed him physically. What they are saying is that if he did not marry you, he wouldn't have died?'

'But why? I don't understand. How?'

'They said you quarrelled with him that morning.'

'The morning he was killed?'

'Yes, the morning he was killed.'

'We did not quarrel mother. We did not.'

'You told him of the dream you dreamt. He did not want to go to work, but you said, "What is in a dream? You are just lazy." So he went and on his way back he met his death.'

'No, no.'

'This is the story. It was circulating during the burial. Mind you, my daughter, I don't believe a word of it. But you can't stop a gossip of this nature.'

'It is more than a gossip. It is wicked, downright wickedness.'

'Did you dream a bad dream before your husband died?'

'Yes, but . . .'

'And did you tell anybody your dream?'

'Yes, I did. A friend. You know her. She cooked many times for me when I had Obii.'

'You did not tell your husband the dream?'

'No, I did not. I was afraid.'

'Well, she added her bit here and there.'

'So, she spread the evil gossip?'

'Well, she was the only person you told your dream.'

Ozoemena found it difficult to believe. What was wrong? Was she getting off her head? If she was not, then all the people around her were getting off their heads too. This would include her mother as well, and her husband's brother. So this is life she said to herself several times. She too was being accused indirectly of killing her husband. And the dream? It was only a dream. She had had so many dreams which were just dreams. But why did she dream that her husband was going on a journey, and it turned out to be that he was really going on a long journey of no return? Was it predicted then that her husband would die? Who predicted it? God? What God? Impossible. It was an accident, true and simple. It could not be anything else. Accident. The lorry driver was careless. He had no brakes, so he crushed her husband while he was returning from work, her husband who was returning to her and his children. But why must it be her husband? Why couldn't it have been another man, another woman's husband. Why was it Chukwuma? Chuk-

77

wuma who came to her school in the company of a friend. It was the friend who had come to see his girl friend. She was merely passing by, and Chukwuma saw her and called her by her name. She did not know him. But he knew her. He also knew her parents.

During the holiday, he proposed to her, and she agreed to marry him. Chukwuma was impatient. She would have liked to do her School Certificate Examination. As it was, she stopped in class four. She had no training of any sort. But it did not worry her. Chukwuma was a loving husband. He took great care of her, and when the children began to arrive, he took even greater care of them. From the onset, it was a happy marriage. She had no cause for regrets.

She was more appreciative of her husband, because he was just an ordinary clerk. He was about four years Ozoemena's senior in school. He was so young, and yet he did not behave in that irresponsible way common to young men of his age. And she was devoted to him. She loved and cherished him. She was determined to pay back by being a good mother and a good wife. In their three years of married life, she thought she was achieving these two qualities, a good wife and a good mother. Then suddenly, without warning, death snatched her husband from her, snatched him away in that cruel way.

He should have been ill. At least four weeks ill and in hospital. That would have given Ozoemena sufficient warning. She would have imagined what it would be to lose her husband. But that cruel way? No, it was too much for her. Too much for her young heart.

And the thought that she dreamed it all. Was that a warning? No. It was not. If it was, it was too short. She couldn't have prevented her husband from going to work that morning. Was he careless? No, he couldn't have been careless. Chukwuma was a careful man. Why then? What then? Why was it Chukwuma and not anybody else? And why did she dream? It reminded her of a story told them by one of the girls in school about an aunt. The girl went on holiday at her aunt's in Enugu. They had arranged to go to

Onitsha one weekend, and she was going with them. But that morning, her aunt woke up not feeling right and, without giving any reasons, ruled that she was not going to Onitsha with them. She was disappointed, but there was nothing she could do.

On their way back from Onitsha, they had an accident. Their car somersaulted three times, and they came out unhurt. Her aunt was treated for shock in the hospital. It was when she was discharged that she revealed her dream to all of them. She had dreamt that the car they were travellling in was full of the blood of her niece. She was trying to bale out the blood with her hands but could not. She did not tell her husband because he would laugh at her. So all she could do was to stop her niece from going with them.

The girl who told them the story was sure that she would have died, or been seriously injured if she had gone with them.

So it was destined after all that we must die at a particular time, and in a particular way. Why do we struggle then? It was all rubbish. Why then did it happen to Chukwuma? Why?

There was no end to this. She was going in circles. Who was she to question all these things?

'Never mind,' she heard her mother saying. 'Some of these things are bound to happen. I am alive. They would have been cruel to you, were I dead. But I am alive. And they will not touch you. Let anybody dare touch you. Uzonwane calls himself a man, let him come. Let him dare come. He will show me he is a man, and I in turn will show him I am a woman. So don't worry, my daughter. You went to school. Things are easier for you children nowadays who went to school. In our time it was quite different. When Uzonwane comes, I am going to deal with him. Let him dare come and molest you, and I'll show him. You are sure that this is all your husband had?'

'If he had anything anywhere, he did not tell me. He died suddenly you know. At the end of each month, he gave me enough money for food and housekeeping. He bought books, for as I told you, he was preparing for an examination.'

'He had no woman anywhere?'

'No,' Ozoemena shouted. How could her mother say a thing like that in this sort of way? How could her husband have had another women? He was faithful to her. He never slept out, was never late in coming home. He did not have bad company. Why did her mother who knew Chukwuma so well talk in that way? What was wrong with these adults?

'I am your mother, do you hear? I carried you in my womb for nine months. I breastfed you. I know the world more than you do. You should start thinking of what you want to do. I don't say don't mourn for your husband. God forbid that I should suggest that. But you should pull yourself together. Think of yourself and your children. You have to bring them up. As I can see it, your husband's brother is not going to do a thing for you. Do you hear my daughter? Have you found out how much your husband had in the bank?'

'Yes.'

'How much?'

'Ten pounds.'

'Ten pounds?'

'Yes,'

'That is all?'

'That is all.'

'Have you told him?'

'Uzonwane?'

'Yes.'

'I have told him.'

'What were his reactions?'

'I don't know.'

'You don't know?'

'I don't know.'

'Did he believe you?'

'That is left to him. I showed him the savings book and his son read it for him.'

80

'What did he do?'

'He asked me to give him the book.'

'Did you give him?'

'Yes. Of course I gave him. There was no alternative.'

'What does he intend to do with it?'

'I don't know. He can't cash it.'

'He can't cash it?'

'No. He can't.'

'Does he know?'

'I suppose so. Why should I worry? It is only ten pounds.'

'Have you ten pounds of your own?'

'No.'

'And you said it is only ten pounds, as if you have a bag of money somewhere. However, what do you intend to do?'

'I have not thought of that yet.'

'You should. It is nearly six weeks since your husband died.'

'I know.'

'Well then.'

'It is difficult to believe.'

'I know. But it must be believed. We must face reality. You understand me. Don't feel I am not sympathetic.'

'I know you are. I know, mother, I know. But please leave me alone. Why don't you all leave me in peace. Please leave me in peace.'

Then her first son came in. He had been playing with the other children on the compound. His nose was running. And he looked rather untidy. He had a pair of shoes on. The other children did not wear shoes. Uzonwane did not see the reason why Chukwuma and his wife should waste money to buy shoes for little children. Shoes made them delicate.

His mother wiped his nose, and rearranged his shirt and shorts, so that he looked tidier. 'Aren't you playing any more?'

'No.'

'Why?' his mother asked.

'Nothing.'

81

'Are you hungry?' The boy shook his head.

'What is the matter then?'

'Nothing.'

'Go and play then.'

'I don't want to play anymore.'

'Are you tired?' The boy said nothing.

'What then?'

'I want to go back to Port Harcourt.'

'I have told you, we shall go back soon.'

'You said so the other day.'

'I said so. But now we shall soon go back.' The boy looked cheerful.

'So that I can start school. Our school has started already. Our teacher will beat me when I start school.'

'She won't beat you. I shall go and explain to her why you were late.'

'Will you?'

'Yes. I will.'

'And will you bring Joe to our school?'

'Yes. I shall take Joe along too.'

'Mummy, when will Joe start school? Daddy said he will start next year. But daddy is dead. When will he start now that daddy is dead?'

'He will start next year. But who told you daddy is dead?'

'I know. You were weeping at Port Harcourt. Aunty was there too. She was weeping and rolling on the floor. They said daddy was dead.'

'So you know.'

'I know. I want to go back to Port Harcourt and go to school.'

'We shall go. I have told you so. But won't you like to go to school here?'

'Here?' he said doubtfully.

'Yes, here. Won't you like to go?' He was not sure. He did not know what it was like to go to school anywhere that was not Port Harcourt.

'I will like to go to school here.'

'Good. That's a good boy. All right, go and play.'

'So this is the way you have brought him up?'

'Yes. Why?'

'To speak in this foreign language. So this is better. This language is better than our own language,' Ozoemena's mother said.

'Mother, how you talk.'

'How do I talk? You have a child, and from the very beginning, you make things difficult for him. Why can't you speak our language to him? Didn't I speak our language to you? Don't you speak the language of the white people well now? You start off your children with a great disadvantage. At this rate, I hope you give them our food to eat.'

'I give them our food.'

'You have done well there. But remember you will have yourself to blame if anything goes wrong in future for them.'

'Nothing will go wrong.'

'Well, it is left to you. What is your plan? I have not asked you.'

'My plan?'

'Yes, your plan. Have you no plan?'

'Isn't it too early to discuss now?'

'Too early? Your children will eat you know.'

'I know.'

'You think I am pushing you too much.'

'No, but . . .'

Yes, plan. She had thought of it. What was she going to do? That was what occupied her mind at the death of her husband. What was she going to do? At first, she was full of regrets. It was barely six years ago that she left school. She remembered it all. She remembered the day the principal of her school called her to talk to her about getting married so early. She had given her an example of a girl who, after two years of married life, decided to go back to school. She was a brilliant girl, but she went on holiday and fell in love with a man who had come home on leave to look for a wife. She did not go back to school. She got married a month later, and

83

after two years, she decided amid protests to go back to school.

Ozoemena stood listening to her principal as she told her this story. It did not make any impression on her. Whoever learnt by someone else's experience? Experience was something personal. It could not be transferred. She knew that what her principal was saying to her meant nothing to her. Her case was quite different. Chukwuma was young and full of promise. What's more, he was able to feed her. Her principal had asked her what she would do if anything happened to her husband and she found out that she had no trade of her own. She remembered her reaction. It was that of indignation. How dared she suggest that sort of thing. What on earth could happen to her fiance? It was wicked of her principal to even think of death.

Her friends in school also warned her, though not as clearly as the principal. Now they were all right and she was wrong. But she did not make a wrong choice. Chukwuma was loving. And she had nothing against him. He was a good, loving and understanding husband. It was fate, it was death that played tricks on her. She could not, no one could fight against death or fate. Her choice was right. It was death that was wrong. She remembered when she had her first son, and how loving her husband was. At night when the baby cried, it was her husband who got up and fed him. He was so helpful. He did not behave like a young father. He was alive to his responsibilities.

If only she got her School Certificate, she would have been sure of a good job. But she had stopped in class four, and that was a great handicap. And she knew that if she had her way, she would go back to school. A teacher training college would do, so that she would be able to look after her children.

'I think I would like to go back to school,' she told her mother.

'School?' her mother asked unbelievingly.

'Yes, to school.'

84

'Is this possible?'

'It is possible if I have the money to pay my fees.'

'You know there is no money.'

'I know.'

'Well then?'

'It is just a wish. If it is possible, I will go back to school. You asked me my plan. That is my plan.'

'And your two sons, who will look after them?'

This came to Ozoemena as a surprise. Was it her mother who asked that question or not. She depended on her. She had assumed that her mother would gladly look after the children.

'You know we don't stay in one place,' her mother said sensing what she was thinking.

'And the school? I wonder who will look after them when I go to the market?'

'That is true. It will be difficult as you can see.'

'It is difficult,' Ozoemena said, wiping the tears from her eyes.

'You are crying again?'

'No, I am not crying.'

'You are. What is this? Wipe your tears. You aren't a child. Wipe your tears quickly. I want you to stay here for a while, and we shall see. I can feed you and your children. By the time the little boy is old enough, something will happen.'

'What will happen?'

'Just be patient, my daughter. You were telling me about Ada. Did she say you could come and stay with her?'

'She said so at first. But I don't know whether she is still keen.'

'Do you like it?'

'I don't. How can I stay with Ada?'

'I thought so. Stay with us.'

'Here?'

'Yes, here. Why do you say so?'

'What will I do here?'

'What will you do in Port Harcourt?' her mother asked.

'I can find a job.'

'With whose help?'

'I have my class four certificate.'

'Isn't it a piece of paper?'

'Yes. I worked for it.'

'You must know someone before you get a job, my daughter. Certificates, or whatever you call them, don't take one anywhere these days.'

As they were talking, someone came in and told Ozoemena's mother that Uzonwane wanted her.

'Can't he come to my house?'

'Mother, go and see him.'

'I want to know whether my house is leaking that he can't come to it. Or that I am too small that it will be undignifying for him to come to my house. All right, tell him I am coming,' she said to the boy who came to call her.

'What does he want me for?' she asked half to herself and half to her daughter.

'Go and find out. You never can tell.'

She sat down after greeting Uzonwane and waited to hear why he called her. He asked her if he would bring kola. She said she did not eat kola. 'Our people met yesterday,' he began. 'On Nkwo day, we would like your daughter to bring out my brother's property, including the bags of money which she hid. Today is Eke. She can go to Port Harcourt tomorrow and bring everything.'

'That's why you called me?' Ozoemena's mother asked. 'My daughter showed you the money in the bank. You are not satisfied with that. All the property that belonged to your brother was brought back by the people you sent to collect them. Still you are not satisfied. I'll deliver your message to my daughter. Thank you.'

'You better do because if you don't, we are going to make her swear by the gods.'

'This is a warning. Thank you.' She got up and went home. That night she brought her daughter, Ozoemena, to her house. She warned her not to discuss with anybody about her late husband until she returned.

In two days Ntianu was back. On the appointed day, she and her daughter and another relation of hers took the savings account of Chukwuma to Uzonwane and his people. Chukwuma's other property was locked up in a room in Uzonwane's house.

'What about the bags of money they said Chukwuma had?' one of the people asked.

'He had no bags of money. If he had he did not tell me before he died,' Ozoemena said almost in tears.

'My daughter, tell us the truth, Uzonwane urged.

'I am telling you the truth,' she said. She was exploding inside her.

'Can you swear by our gods?' one asked.

'I can swear on anything,' she said.

'If you know where these bags of money are, why not reveal it? Why torture the little girl of yesterday who lost such a husband?' Ntianu's relative said. 'Is it just hearsay or what?'

'We know what we are doing,' Uzonwane said. Ntianu said nothing.

Nobody said anything for a while. Uzonwane shifted uncomfortably in his seat. 'Our people, we have to disperse now. My daughter, we give you four days to tell us where the money is. If you don't tell us then we shall make you swear by the gods. Our people, isn't it so?'

'It is so,' the people said.

Ozoemena went out one evening with her two children when somebody came to visit her and her mother. From the way her mother received the visitor, it was obvious that she expected him.

After the kola, she gave him a large bottle of stout. The man was sipping it when Ozoemena came in. The man got up from the chair he sat on. 'This my daughter, Ozoemena,' she said. She greeted him shyly and went into the room. The man sat down again and continued talking with Ozoemena's mother. When he was about to leave, Ozoemena's mother called her. She came out, greeted him again and disappeared.

At night Ntianu called her daughter. 'You saw that man?'

'Yes,' Ozoemena said. 'He is a big man. He is going to help you get admission into a college of your choice.'

'Will he?'

'Yes. I went to see him a few days ago. I told him about you and he is ready to help.'

'Can he get me into college next year?'

'Yes of course. He can do that easily for you.'

'Who is he, mother?'

Ntianu did not reply for some time. The question came to her as a surprise. She did not think her daughter was going to ask her that question. Therefore she did not have a ready answer. What was she going to say to her? 'He works at Aba. Don't you know him?'

'No, I don't know him. Never seen him before.'

'I know him very well. He was a good friend of your father. And he wants to help you. In a week or so, you'll go to Aba to see him. Meanwhile, give me all the clothes and cloths and presents your late husband gave you. I'll return all of them to Uzonwane.'

'No.'

'I'll return all of them to him. They are bad people. If you don't return them, their gods would harm you.'

'Even the wedding ring?'

'Even the wedding ring.'

Ozoemena got ready and went to Aba. She did not find it difficult to locate the man's house. When she knocked, the door was opened by a little girl of about seven years old. 'Is Mr. Azubike in?' Ozoemena asked timidly.

'Papa is not in, but Mama is in,' the girl said opening the door wider. Ozoemena went in and sat down. A woman came out and greeted her. 'My husband will soon come back,' she said to her.

She waited for nearly an hour before Mr. Azubike returned.

'This is Ntianu's daughter,' he said to his wife. '*Ewoo* my daughter. You lost your husband at Port Harcourt. Sorry, my daughter. These drivers and recklessness, making such a young girl a widow. Sorry. How are your children?'

'They are well,' Ozoemena replied.

'Fancy, not recognising you. I know your mother very well. When we finish eating, we shall go and see the people for your admission,' Mr. Azubike said.

In the evening, Ozoemena found herself in a fabulous sitting room. There was a little man sitting in one of the chairs. Both the chair and the dress he wore did not make much difference to his size. Mr. Azubike bowed low to the little man, and to Ozoemena's dismay, left the room.

What was she going to say to the man? How was she to begin?

'Come nearer,' she heard the man saying. She was afraid to go nearer. 'Come nearer,' the man encouraged. 'I am not going to eat you up.' She went nearer. He took hold of a telephone that was beside him, dialled a number and began to speak. Ozoemena was a little relaxed as she heard him mention the college she wanted to go, admission, fees and all that. 'I'll send her to you tomorrow,' he said and hung up. 'You'll start in January. I shall pay all the fees for the three years in advance.' He rang a bell and a steward came in with different kinds of assorted drinks. Ozoemena took a soft drink. 'Take brandy,' the man said.

'No, thank you. I don't know how to drink it,' Ozoemena said. She was taken aback by what the man had just said. She was a child as well as a mother. But she understood what it all meant. She became very uncomfortable. the man watched her with interest. He was mysterious to Ozoemena. She knew that he was an old hand in this sort of thing from the way he watched her. He seemed to tell her, 'That's how they all behave at first. You'll be all right when we start. It will be fun when we start.'

'Where is the college situated in Aba?' Ozoemena finally asked.

'One or two miles from here. The driver will take you to

school every morning. Don't worry about the distance.' Ozoemena wanted to ask where she would live, then she changed her mind. The question was pointless. She knew. 'So that's how it happens, so that's the beginning of the journey of no return? So that's how girls get hooked?' she thought. Then she looked at the man, and the whole thing became unbearable. It was so revolting to her. Her mother, so she knew. So she planned this, her own mother? It is not possible. Her own mother who gave birth to her? She heard that women used girls in this way, but she did not know that a mother could use her own daughter in this way as well.

'I want to go,' she said getting up.

'You want to go? You are such an interesting little girl. We shall be friends. Never mind.' He fumbled in his pocket, and brought out some notes. 'This is for you,' he said giving it to Ozoemena. 'You are going so early. Are you upset? We haven't even talked about the school. Never mind. We shall talk about that when I come to see you at your mother's.'

'At my mother's, you will come to my mother?' Ozoemena asked.

'Yes, why do you ask that question? You children, you are all the same. You will be all right. When you come again, I wouldn't like to see you in that black you are wearing. It is unnecessary. This is a new age, mind you.' He realised that he was still holding the notes, that Ozoemena had not taken them from him. 'Won't you take the money?'

'Why should you insult me in this way?' Ozoemena finally asked. 'What is my sin? Why do you want to exploit me because I lost my husband, and it would seem, have no means of livelihood. Haven't you a grown-up daughter? Would you like her to be thus treated if she married and lost her husband in a motor accident?'

'What are you talking about? Don't you want to get married again?'

'Get married to you, to you because you are wealthy, because you'll send me to college, because . . . because . . .' She burst out into inconsolable tears.

'You have come back quickly,' Ozoemena's mother said. She did not answer her. She went in and saw her children. They were sleeping. The elder boy looked like her late husband when he was sleeping. 'What exactly did you want me to go and do at Aba?' Ozoemena asked her mother. She was surprised at her boldness. Her head was high. She did not care a hoot now. Her mother became worried. 'What do you mean?' she asked. 'What did you mean by asking me to go to Aba?' she repeated her question.

'I would have thought that if I wanted to be a prostitute, I should go about it my own way, without the aid or the connivance of my own mother. And that . . .' She choked.

Her mother collected her in her arms. 'My daughter, I meant no harm. Please forgive me. Please forgive me. It was for your own good . . .'

'For my own good? To live with such a man, with such a reputation, so he would send me to college? I don't deserve this mother. Oh God, why did you allow my husband to die? Chukwuma, why, why . . .'

There was a knock at the door. Ntianu opened it. Ozoemena tried to collect herself. A little boy came in. 'Uzonwane said they went to a *dibia* and he told them that the bags of money were hidden somewhere in Port Harcourt. If Ozoemena still denied any knowledge of them, she must swear by our gods tomorrow before the sun was up.'

91

# The Loss of Eze

Tunde came to my life when I lost Eze. I did not lose him through death. Someone, a woman, snatched him away from me. I thought my heart would break when I lost Eze. He was everything to me. He had seen my father when he visited me in Lagos. He had told him about us, and my father, though not too happy, consented. He wanted me to settle down. All my sisters had settled down, and were with their husbands and children. I wasn't too keen on settling down. I had lots of boy friends when I was at school, and by the time I left the University, and worked for two years I saw that all my sweethearts had settled down and had families. I was too choosy.

My interests were diverse, and I was never bored until I lost Eze. It was an affair that took everything out of me. The fire that burned inside me in those one and a half years of love was a consuming fire. I didn't know it would ever be quenched. I thought it would burn forever. Eze said it would burn forever and I believed him. It burned for only eighteen months, and when it was quenched, nothing could rekindle it. We tried for a little while after our friends had intervened, but the firewood was too wet.

For six whole months, I did not know what to do with myself. You are lost when you suddenly find yourself left out, when you suddenly discover that you have lost someone who was life itself to you. You grope in darkness, you ask yourself so many questions which you can't answer, or questions whose answers frighten you. You are empty inside you, and you want to fill this emptiness depending of course on the kind of person you are. I was sensitive as a child, I think I still am. At first I was gripped with fear, fear of the world, fear of human beings, fear of all around me. The fear was getting too much, it was getting me. I was losing my self-confidence, a quality I thought I had in abundance. And that was what really frightened me and made me shake myself, and say, many times over, 'Amede come out of it, come out of it before you are destroyed.' I said this aloud to myself, I said it in my dreams, I said it everywhere.

So after six months of losing Eze I said to hell with him. To hell with all I held dear, I must live my own life the way I wanted it. Eze or no Eze, I must live my life fully and usefully. That week, I got an invitation from one of the embassies. I was on their list. That meant that any time there was a party or something I was invited to it. One of them had even told me once when an invitation for me came late, and I was not at the party, that I did not need to wait to receive invitations. When I heard of anything, I should jump into my car and come. It was kind and well meaning, I knew, but how many people would do that without embarrassment of a sort?

I looked forward to this party, in the way I hadn't looked forward to many parties. I didn't know why. Perhaps it was because of my state of mind, it was because of Eze; perhaps it was because of loneliness. I was lonely. I had shut myself out of the world that was around me, without knowing it. Now I was going out again to take my share of it. My share! I shuddered as the word 'share' came to my mind. Wasn't it because some people wanted their 'fair share' of wealth, without contributing to this wealth that left the country in such a mess, that ushered in military rule, that had led to so much bloodshed and suffering. No, I mustn't use that word again. I must go into the world, and seize the bull by the horn. The world, in many respects, was a bull. A mighty bull. You couldn't even seize it by its horns. The horns were too many and too dangerous to come near to.

In preparation for the party, I went to the hairdresser to

93

have my wig done. Sam was there. He came forward and shook my hand, happy to see me. 'Did you travel, madam?' he asked me. He hadn't seen me for over six months. In those days with Eze, Sam saw me in the hairdressing saloon twice a month. Eze was fussy about my appearance. So I made sure my wigs were done twice a month. I had two at the time, and was contemplating having a third one when Eze left me.

'I was abroad,' I lied to Sam, and gave him my wig. 'Any style you like,' I said. I never selected a style. I trusted Sam to select for me. And he always satisfied me. Once I selected a style, Eze so criticised it that I went back to have it redone.

'Do you want it tonight?' Sam asked.

'Not tonight. On Saturday. I shall come at four on Saturday.'

'We are normally busy on Saturday afternoons. What about Saturday morning?' I said it was all right. I would leave the office before eleven. There was usually not much work on Saturdays in the office.

The party was at nine o'clock. At eight, I started getting ready. It was my first Saturday night out in six months. With Eze, we went out every Saturday night. We ate out, and then went to dance. When I did not fully like it, we stayed at home and watched the late Saturday television film which was usually good.

I wore some old clothes which I liked very much, and watched the effect it had in the mirror. To my consternation, I saw that I had lost weight considerably. Gaining and losing weight came to me easily, depending on my mind. When I slept well, I ate well, and gained weight. When I slept poorly, I ate poorly, and lost weight. That night, I discovered that I had steadily lost weight. I was all bone, and no flesh. This was not the kind of appearance I wanted to have, if I was going to say, to hell with Eze, and people like Eze. I called my cook-steward and asked him to prepare supper quickly. He said, 'Yes madam,' and went to the kitchen. My cook-steward never asked questions. He took orders only. I had said that I did not want supper barely an hour before.

I removed the dress, and looked for something else to wear from the wardrobe. Wrappa would be a better dress to wear, not a frock. I looked for one blue one I had made nearly five years ago. My mother had altered the top for me. I called my steward to have it ironed for me. I had a pair of drop blue earrings. I fished them out. By this time, it was nine thirty. That did not bother me. 'Never be in a hurry when you are going to a party,' I heard Esther saying to me. That was what she always said to me, when I hurried for a party. 'Parties should be enjoyed fully, and that means you must go to them relaxed and radiant.' I smiled when I remembered her. She was at the moment in Britain. She went to do a course in architecture for six months. She had been away for two months, and she hadn't written yet. She had told me when I told her about Eze, 'When one door closes, another one opens.' At the time, I thought that was an oversimplification of my problem. And besides, we were two different people. She had already taken the bull by its dangerous horns, and had said to hell with everything.

To my surprise the wrappa looked nice. It did something for me, the way that the dress did nothing for me. I wore the blue earrings. My neck was bare. I thought of a gold chain and pendant. No, that would not do. I'd rather have on the pair of blue earrings with no gold chain. I was satisfied with the look. I took my handbag and locked my bedroom, half thinking that Eze might be in the sitting room waiting for me. The food was ready. I sat down, and ate for five minutes and went out.

'If you wait until midnight, and I don't return, go to bed,' I said to my steward. 'Yes madam,' he replied. It was always 'yes madam'. 'Madam' was getting on my nerves these days. In the office, in the shops, in the streets, people called you 'madam'. Even in Biafra, there was something like 'Tick madam'! I had thought of asking my steward to call me Miss Ezeka. I should tell him the following day.

There were hundreds of cars. I parked and walked up to the house. 'Good evening, Miss Ezeka.' I turned, and there was Mr. Smith. 'Quite an age,' he said. 'Yes quite an age. How is life?' I said. We shook hands and walked into the house together.

The guest of honour was at the door with the hostess. I knew the hostess very well. 'This is Miss . . .' 'I know Miss Ezeka,' the guest of honour said. I was elated. I felt my confidence returning. I went to the table to have something to drink. Mr. Smith followed me. He asked me what I wanted to drink and I said gin and tonic. I sipped it. It was Eze who taught me how to drink gin and tonic. What I drank before I met him was gin and lime. He convinced me that gin and tonic was more sophisticated. Eze was very sophisticated. I didn't know whether that was why I fell in love with him. He wasn't handsome. But he was dark, the complexion I liked, and he dressed very well. Whether in suit or in casuals, he was always the best dressed anywhere.

What a crowd. The orchestra was playing. But guests were not dancing at the time. I sipped my gin and tonic, and talked to Mr. Smith. Then someone I didn't know, I hadn't seen before joined us.

'I don't think you have met,' Mr. Smith said.

'No,' I said.

The stranger smiled. 'We haven't met, but I know you are Miss Ezeka, and you work in the Bureau of Publicity and . . .' He stopped. My word, what was he going to say next?

Mr. Smith began to talk. 'I need not introduce you then,' he said in his shy way. The stranger gripped the hand I did not outstretch, and shook it. 'I am Mr. Bright of the Western Bureau of Publicity. I have heard so much about you.'

'In what connection, may I ask,' I said slowly but firmly. I was losing my temper. What brazenness. Mr. Smith took leave of us. Obviously, he sensed what was going to happen next, and he was not prepared for a scene of any nature. 'Never mind in what connection. Let's go and dance.'

'No thank you. This is not the time to dance. Tell me, in what connection. I would like to know. I work in the Bureau of Publicity all right,' I insisted.

'I know Eze,' he said laughing.

'You do, do you? What is funny about that?'

'And I have been wanting to meet you, but Eze wouldn't let me.'

'I see.' Then someone joined us. He was a stranger. I was struck by his neat appearance. 'How are you Tunde? Meet Miss Ezeka.' I shook his hand, and smiled 'Nice to meet you, Miss Ezeka. I am Tunde Abiola. I work at the D.T.C.'

'Let me go and get you something to drink,' Mr. Bright said. 'Allow me,' Tunde said, and took my glass. 'Gin and tonic,' I said to him.

Mr. Bright did not leave my side. Then I saw my boss' wife, and excused myself. I went to her and greeted her. She was a polite woman, not beautiful, but very attractive. 'Amede, so you are here. I trust you,' she said in her usual soft way. 'Where is Eze?' she asked. 'Is he here with you? You two are inseparables.' My God, not here. Hadn't she heard? Didn't her husband tell her? He did not, otherwise she would not torment me in this way. She was not that type of person. She wasn't doing it deliberately. She did not know. Before I answered, Tunde came with my drink. I took it gratefully and introduced him to my boss' wife. They shook hands, and she left to join the wives who had now carved out a section for themselves the unmarried ones like us dared not go near. At such parties, the husbands and the bachelors and the bachelor girls stood talking in groups of threes and fives and sixes.

'Would you like to sit down?' Tunde asked me.

'No,' I said. I didn't want to sit down.

'You work in the Bureau of Publicity?'

'Yes.'

'They are doing very useful work,' Tunde said.

'Oh, thank you,' I said.

'You sent me very useful information when I was abroad. I think it was you who signed the letter. I remember it was a feminine hand.'

'I might have,' I said. 'I sign many letters every day in the office. How is the politics in the D.T.C.?' He laughed but before he replied Mr. Bright joined us again.

'This is a wretched country,' he said. 'Damnable country. Day in day out, parties. A friend who recently returned from Britain, after going to four parties in one night, asked me when Nigeria did her thinking. I told him that nobody thought in Nigeria.'

'In Lagos,' I said.

'In Lagos,' Mr. Bright said. 'I can talk of Lagos. You are right, Amede.' How impudent of him to call me by my name, and to pronounce it like that.

'I guess you don't know Ibadan?' Tunde asked. He said it in such a way that made me believe he was either from Ibadan, or he knew Ibadan very well.

'Never set my foot there. When I came back from Britain, and got this job in the W.B.P. I was told to go to Ibadan. I resigned right away. I told them they could keep their job. An uncle intervened. Someone else was transferred to Ibadan, I believe a son of the soil. I remained in Lagos. How can any sane person live out of Lagos?'

'You mean you have not been to the North and the East?' Tunde asked.

'Have you been to the East?' I asked Tunde.

'Not since I returned from Britain not quite eighteen months ago. I shall go to the East again when I have my leave.'

'So you have been to the East before?' Mr. Bright said.

'I went to the East when I was at school. I had an uncle in Port Harcourt, a goldsmith. I took a very old boat from Apapa to Port Harcourt. I spent a week in Port Harcourt. Then I took a train to Enugu, from there back to Lagos. I would very much like to visit Onitsha. I have heard to much about it from my friends in the D.T.C. and even when I was abroad,' Tunde concluded. My estimation of him rose high. Here is someone who is different from the others. Here is someone who did not think that Lagos was the centre of the universe.

98

'I shall go home in a month's time. Would you like to come with me?' I asked Tunde. He smiled before he answered.

'You don't believe me,' he said.

'Oh I believe you,' I said. Indeed I believed him.

'How long would it take you to travel to the East? Six days?' Mr. Bright asked in his best intonation. Tunde smiled a knowing smile.

'It will take me six days. How clever of you,' I laughed. 'When I leave Lagos at six in the morning in my car . . .'

'You will drive for six days?' Mr. Bright asked. He did not understand.

'Yes. I would leave Lagos at six. Spend the night at Ibadan, travel the following morning to Ondo, then the third day spend the night at Ore, the fourth night at Benin, and . . .' Tunde could not help laughing aloud now. What ignorance, he seemed to say in his laughter.

'Mr. Bright,' Tunde said. 'It would take Miss Ezeka about seven hours to travel to Onitsha.'

'Seven hours. Impossible. You don't mean it. That jungle, in seven hours, the roads? I don't believe it.'

'There is the new road recently opened. I understand it is a good road. The old road is good too.'

'Still I don't believe it.'

'Didn't you do geography at school?' I asked.

'I did geography of course.'

'You did the geography of Nigeria?'

'We did the geography of the British Isles, Canada, Australia and New Zealand and . . . .'

'What are you people talking about? Book? Miss Ezeka, wherever you are you talk nothing but book. Let's go and dance. Oh, that's Mr. Abiola. How do you do? So you are at this party? Ah, Mr. Bright, "Okunri meta". Didn't I say there were so many distinguished people at this party. Let's go and dance Miss Ezeka. I shall bring her back, gentlemen.' The gentlemen bowed as my boss took me to the floor. Tunde went to the table and got me a gin and tonic. Mr.

Bright went to dance.

The only lady he saw to dance with was my boss's wife. He went to her, bowed low. But she shook her head. 'I have a bad leg,' she whispered into his ear. Mr. Bright felt hurt and went over to Tunde, who was now talking to a white woman, holding two drinks on both hands.

'Shall we dance?' Mr. Bright asked the woman.

'Certainly,' she said. She was handing her drink to Tunde, who raised the two glasses he held for her to see. 'Oh,' she said. Mr. Bright looked on. 'Darling do hold this,' she said to a white man who was obviously her husband.

Tunde sat down at an empty table as he waited for me to return. I watched him as I danced. My boss was just being formal. He dreaded women. And he thought I would be annoyed with him if he did not dance with me. He wasn't a dancer anyway. So we talked all the time, moving our legs. There were so many people on the floor. Gay couples dancing and laughing under the bright light. Some girls came out and sang. They sang beautifully.

'So you know Mr. Bright,' my boss said to me.

'I met him for the first time tonight,' I said.

'I see,' he said, and continued dancing. I took the hint at once.

'Shall we exchange partners sir?' Mr. Bright said.

'Oh, we are going to sit down,' my boss said. 'The lady says she has danced enough. Delicate creatures.'

Tunde came to meet us with my glass. My boss left him to take care of me and went to his wife for a dance. I was glad to sit down. And I took a deep drink.

'If you are serious about taking me to Onitsha, I shall take a casual leave and go with you,' Tunde said.

'Never mind, there is plenty of time.'

'Are you serious?' Tunde asked. The way he asked, the anxiety on his face, showed me that I had, without knowing it, committed myself. 'Plenty of time,' what did I mean by 'plenty of time'? And how clever of him to jump at the words.

'Well, plenty of time,' I said smiling.

100

'You haven't told me about the politics in the D.T.C.,' I said.

'There is nothing to tell. I am new in the place. Only eighteen months. I have not found myself in a faction yet.'

'So it is true there are two factions.'

'There are two factions,' he said, 'and you must belong to one.'

'You mean you can't be neutral?' I asked wanting to confirm what I had heard already.

'No, you cannot be neutral,' Tunde said.

One man had likened the place to a drunkard who was returning home after midnight, dead drunk. On his way, he met a ghost who said to him: 'If you dance, you will be killed; if you don't dance, you will be killed.' The drink cleared from the drunkard's eyes, and he said: 'I shall dance, I shall not dance, I shall dance, I shall not dance.'

'You must be involved in it somehow,' I said smiling.

'Yes, somehow,' Tunde said. 'And from what I have seen, both factions are equally guilty. We spend precious time on irrelevant things. The job is left undone. The junior workers are dissatisfied with their seniors, and the seniors with one another. There is no organisation whatever in the damn place. And I believe that the longer you stay there, the more rustic you become. What they do night and day, is intrigue, and counter intrigue. Nothing constructive, nothing challenging. I was thinking of setting up something on my own, but I haven't got the capital . . . Let's go and dance. I am talking too much.'

We went to dance. We met Mr. Bright on the way. 'I must go now,' he said. 'My boys and I are going to interview a distinguished personality at the airport. We are almost late. Expect my call on Monday, Amede. Tell your telephone operators that you are expecting an important call, and that the person would not want to be kept waiting.'

Tunde and I went on dancing. I looked at my watch, and it was nearly midnight. Many people had gone, but many more remained. Drinks were still flowing. 'How long have you been in Lagos?' Tunde asked me.

'This is my sixth year,' I said.

'You are a Lagos girl then,' he said.

'No, I am not a "Lagos girl." I work in Lagos. I don't really belong here. And to qualify for a "Lagos girl", you must really belong to Lagos. You must cast off all decency, scrape your eyebrows sort of. That's the meaning of the phrase, "Lagos girl". It does not mean someone who has lived in Lagos for twenty or fifteen years. But you are an old boy of King's, you should know.'

'Like you, I don't belong here. All my holidays were spent at home.'

'Where is home?'

'Can you guess?'

'Ibadan?'

'No. Guess again.'

'Abeokuta? Ijebu?'

'No, I am not from Ijebu. I am from Ado-Ekiti,' he said.

'Yes, up-country. Eko people make fun of us. They say we are bush people, uncivilised.'

'Eko people like Mr. Bright,' I said.

'Yes, Eko people like Mr. Bright,' Tunde repeated, smiling. 'They tell you they are not really Yorubas, but Brazillians. Their ancestors and themselves travelled throughout Europe. Many of them have not been to Ibadan, not to mention outlandish places like Ado-Ekiti. Let me get you something to drink,' he said. He went off to get me something to drink, and I sat waiting for him. Presently I realised that Tunde had been with me all the evening. It didn't seem as if he came with anybody. Perhaps he wasn't married. He had returned home only eighteen months ago. I had never seen him in these parties. But then, how could I see anybody at that time, when Eze was my life. I saw no one. It may have been that Tunde was at the parties and I did not notice him. For he did not notice me.

He came back with a glass of gin and tonic. He touched my outstretched hand as he gave me the glass.

'What are you drinking? I have not asked you,' I said.

'Gin and tonic,' he said. I took his glass and tasted it. It was Seven Up.

'No alcohol?' I asked.

'No, I don't drink. I go to parties to meet nice people, not to drink.'

'I don't go to parties to drink, though I drink gin and tonic,' I said.

'I know. I don't drink. I sometimes drink half a bottle of beer when I am thirsty, not more.'

'My boss is still dancing. He must be in the mood tonight. And I can't go before him,' I said.

'That's good etiquette,' Tunde said. 'I am lucky my boss is not at the party. I would have been compelled to wait until he left. Let's go and dance.'

We went to the floor and began dancing. It was indeed an enjoyable party. Tunde had made it so for me. I am sure that but for him, I would have gone home long ago, boss or no boss. Mr. Bright had gone a long time ago. There were quite a few people now. Many of them were sitting down. There was still some eatables on the tables. I told Tunde I wanted to eat. We stopped dancing, and went to the table. Some meat rolls had just been brought on the table. They were hot and fresh. I ate several as we were standing.

'I must go,' I announced. So we finished our drinks and went to the door. The host and the hostess were not at the door now. They were sitting down. They were at the door two and a half hours before. I didn't stop wondering what foreigners thought of Lagos people. A cocktail didn't stop at eight fifteen but went on until ten o'clock. A reception went on until the early hours of the morning.

We said thank you to them and walked into the darkness. 'Where did you park?' Tunde said to me.

'Down the road,' I said. He followed me to my car, opened the car for me, and said he would drive behind me. I was a bit taken aback when he said that. Lagos men. All of them were the same. There was nothing I could do. I drove slowly.

Before I came to the crossroads, I heard a horn, and I knew he was following me.

I parked in the garage and came out. He parked behind my car. 'So you live in this posh place. I have been here before and had seen your car. I never knew I would have the privilege to meet its owner.'

We climbed the stairs. It was past two in the morning. I opened the door and we entered. 'You are safe now. I must go. I'll see you tomorrow. Do you think you will be up before eleven?'

'I shall be up before seven, but perhaps go to bed again if I have nothing interesting to do,' I said feeling happy. Oh, he was such a nice person. He did not want to be funny like other Lagos men. He was different after all.

'I shall call at ten in the morning then. Would you like to go on a drive?'

'Yes,' I said, yawning.

'Good night. You are tired. See you tomorrow at ten.' He shook my hand and went down the stairs. I locked the door, and went to my bedroom. I looked at myself in the mirror. I felt pleased. I still looked presentable. I didn't, like other females, go to the washroom to freshen up every other hour. I didn't take to that habit. It wasn't a good habit especially when you had someone beside you who cared.

I looked at my dress. Though it was old, it wasn't bad at all. It hid my thin figure. I changed into my nightie, went to the bathroom to wash my feet in cold water, and my face as well. I rubbed olive oil on my feet and face, and went into bed.

I suddenly woke up and looked at the time. It was only four o'clock. Why did I wake up? Was I troubled? It must be excitement. Excitement at meeting Tunde or what? He was nice. He did not say anything to me. He cared for me at the party, that was all. And he brought me home. He was so nice, the nicest person I had ever met. So I said when I met Eze. How did I lose Eze? Up till now, I could not understand it.

I closed my eyes. I was dancing with Tunde. Mr. Bright

was dancing with a white woman. 'Can we exchange partners?' Mr. Bright said. 'No,' Tunde replied. 'We are going to sit down. Miss Ezeka is tired.' I opened my eyes again. It was six in the morning. In four hours, it would be ten o'clock.

# A Soldier Returns Home

His plane had probably taken off before the rebels seized the airport. Two soldiers had come to see him in at the Kaduna airport. One was his driver. The other one he had not seen before. He was observant. There was something that was disquieting about his driver. At first he did not lay his hand on anything. Afterwards he knew.

His driver greeted him in the way he had not done before. When they reached his house at the barracks he gave few instructions and went in. He was a bachelor. The cook was nowhere to be found. The house was empty. But that was not new. The house was always empty. He did not mind. He just slept there, and he slept when he was very tired, after the day's work. So the emptiness of the room did not matter to him. But that day, it did.

So he phoned a girl friend. It was a girl he had picked up not quite two months ago. She answered. Thank goodness. 'When did you come home darling?' she asked. 'A little while ago . . . darling,' he said. Darling, when did Amina start calling him darling? he thought. Never before had she called him darling. And he, for all he knew, had never called her darling until now. 'Coming round this night?' he asked. She hesitated. And he wondered. She never hesitated. She always came when he wanted her. Both knew what they wanted each other for, and there was no pretence about it. It did not seem as if he thought about her when she was not with him. As for her, he thought that she was incapable of any thoughts. He sometimes, in those sober moments, thought he was a bit unfair, but there was nothing he could do about it. 'I can't make it,' she said. 'Mother is ill,' she said after a pause. Who was mother? Amina had never mentioned mother at any time. He had mentioned his mother once, and she laughed at him. 'A man like you talking about mother as if you were a little girl.' 'I won't press,' he heard himself saying. 'I shall see you tomorrow night then. I am a bit tired after the trip, and the hectic parties in Lagos. I think, I'll just have a bath, go down to the mess, have a beer or two and go to bed.'

'That's a good boy. See you tomorrow then.'

'You are not cutting me off, are you? You haven't told me what you have been doing with yourself since I was away.'

'I've been a good girl,' Amina said, and he laughed. How could Amina be a good girl? It was not possible. She was good in only one thing, sex. And that was all he wanted from her. He knew she had so many men in her life, but in recent times, she was getting more and more attached to him, and this was frightening him. He did not want to be bugged down in Kaduna with a semi-illiterate woman. 'See you tomorrow then,' Amina said again.

'OK! If you so wish. My regards to your mother.'

Okay hung up and sat down in the chair in the sitting room. He looked at the time, and saw that it was only seven in the evening. He tuned the radio, got a station that played a classical piece and sat back to listen to it. Then the face of his driver came back to him. He looked agitated, there was no question about it. Why was he so agitated? And he did not even hang around to see whether he would be of any use, as normally did. They were best of friends. Okay did not believe in the master-servant relationship. He believed in treating everybody great or small humanely.

As he was running his bath, there was a knock on the door. He hadn't gone into the bath yet, so he came out in his dressing gown. His cook hadn't returned. It was the driver. He saluted, and spoke: 'There is trouble, run for your life.' That was all he said in Hausa. He saluted again. Okay stared at him. He turned, and left. Okay got up. He called him. He turned and walked up to him. He stretched his hand and shook the driver's, and said thank you.

That was all he needed to be told. He had suspected it for a long time, but he was afraid to discuss it with any of his comrades in arms. It was a delicate issue. What was he going to do? Escape, that was all he was going to do, plan to escape. He did not know when the rebels would strike. He forgot to have his bath. He called his cook, and there was no answer. He was still not home. He went to a colleague. He wasn't in. He went to another. He had travelled to Kano. His boss was the next one he called on. If they were going to strike, they would strike at dead of night.

Okay waited for his boss in the sitting room. The house used to be filled with children. Now, they had all gone home with their mother, and his boss, like him, was a bachelor. He was in the good books of his boss, or so he thought. He nearly always bought drinks for him in the mess, and he had done his work well.

He greeted him as he came out from the bedroom. There was no time to waste. There was nobody at hearing distance. So he told him exactly what his driver had told him.

'Why didn't you arrest him?' his boss said. Okay was taken aback. What was his boss talking about? Arrest his driver who had told him such a thing, such useful information? He used to think better of his boss. Now he did not know what he thought.

'I couldn't have arrested him. I wasn't armed, and I would have been shot. He did not come alone.'

'Who came with him?'

'I don't know sir. He came up, told me what he had to say, and went away.'

The boss sat without speaking for a while. Okay got up. He fidgeted for a little while and said he was going. He left.

Back in the house, he went straight into the bedroom, and sat down on the bed. What could he do? He must escape. This he knew he must do. He wasn't going to wait and get shot in his bed. But why?

He sat, thinking. Then he was conscious of something

108

creeping under his feet. He jumped up, and went for his revolver. Then he looked down. It was water. He had left the tap running, and now there was water all over the bedroom. Both the bathroom and the toilet were full of water. Then he remembered. It no longer frightened him. He went to the bathroom and turned off the tap. Without thinking of it, he removed his clothes and went into the bath. He came out and wore his uniform. This did not take him time at all. He had a few pounds in the house, so he took them and put them in his pocket. What next? His passbook. There wasn't much there. He took it, took his passport and file. The file contained the letters of his fiancee, who was in Lagos. What next? He went to the kitchen. There was food cooking in the gas stove. It was burning. His cook had come back, started cooking, and then went out again. Was he being watched? Didn't he know that he was home? What was happening? He left some money on the kitchen table for the cook. It was his salary for the month that would end in a few days.

He went to the sitting room, sat down, and lighted his cigarette. It did not taste good in his mouth, so he threw it away. Where was he going? He was all dressed up. What was his boss doing? He did not take him seriously. Perhaps nothing was going to happen, and he would merely look foolish. A soldier, running away. He shouldn't run away. He should stay and see it through. If they would start shooting, they would come for him at night. Many would come for him. If he managed to get one or two, the others would get him. There was no question about that, and he wasn't a gunner as such. He was a pilot. Escape. He must alert one or two people more. And get killed in the process? His boss did not think there was something wrong. Was it the others who would take him seriously?

He fell asleep, and when he woke up, it was ten o'clock. He woke up, because he heard the sound of a plane. It was so loud and it went past his roof. That was strange. Planes didn't normally take that route. Plane, that's it. He must escape in a plane. There was a plane he was so fond of. He had flown it several times to Lagos and Enugu on official business.

He waited. Then it was eleven. What was he waiting for in fact? Waiting to be killed? He went down and hailed a taxi. It stopped. 'Airport,' he said.

'Airport this dead of night? I don't go to the airport at night, master.'

'I'll wait for another taxi then,' Okay said. The taxi driver drove away, then came back after going about a hundred yards. 'Will you pay one pound?'

'Go to hell. I am going to pay the normal fare which is five shillings.' His fear was leaving him. He could see a kind of new life coming into him. 'If you will take five shillings, take it. If not go along, and don't obstruct another taxi.'

'What I am saying is that you are not likely to get any other taxi. They have gone to bed.' Okay wasn't listening to him now. He was walking towards the airport. It was six miles away. It was then that it occurred to him that he should have taken his car. No, that wasn't wise. Everybody knew his car. They would shoot him at sight if they saw him in his car. His car would wait.

The taxi driver pulled up in front of him and asked him to jump in. He got into the front seat. He lighted his cigarette and he was able to see the face of the taxi driver now. Then he smiled. 'I know your master, you know,' he said.

'It is true, sir. It was when you spoke that I recognised your voice. Why are you going to the airport at this dead of night?'

'Is your master at home?' Okay asked instead. Another idea was taking shape in his head.

'My master left ages ago. He first sent home his wives and children, then his property, and then flew to Port Harcourt. He said he was through with Kaduna. He came to Kaduna as a young man. Now he was old.'

'And are you planning to go home?'

'Not when I have not made the money. This taxi belongs to me now. My master sold it to me. He asked me if I could

110

take a risk. I said I would, so he sold it to me at half the price. When did one take a risk, if not when one was young? I couldn't take a risk in my old age.'

Okay wasn't listening anymore. His head was reeling. There were all sorts of plans. He seemed to be abandoning the plan of taking the plane. Then he asked the taxi driver if he would take him to the railway station instead. The driver was surprised. Why the railway station when he had said the airport? There was no passenger train at the railway station. He said he would take a goods train.

'But where are you going in the first place?' the taxi driver asked.

'Drive on. Drive on to the airport.'

They arrived at the airport. It was quiet as usual at that time of day. He spoke briefly to some one on duty, and did not wait for an answer. The plane was not there. He was daft he thought. He had been away for the past fortnight, and had only arrived back that evening. He hadn't even checked the plane on his arrival, and he had taken all the trouble to come to the airport. And in any case, he should not be in a military dress at that time. The more he thought about the impending trouble, the more he believed that there would be trouble. It was becoming more real every minute.

The taxi driver was waiting for him. He jumped into the taxi, and asked the driver to go to the railway station. 'Is there something wrong?' he asked.

'All is not well. I want to go home, that's all, and if you can, you should go home too.'

'You mean home in the East?' 'Yes,' Okay said.

'I haven't made it yet,' he said.

'Made what?'

'Money,' the taxi driver said. 'I came here only five years ago. My master spent nearly thirty years here.'

'That is true,' Okay said. 'That is very true.'

In a short time, they were at the railway station. He paid him and wished him well. There was no train, but the station master was expecting a goods train in an hour. An hour

111

passed then two, and there was no train. Okay was asleep on a chair. Then someone woke him up. It was the taxi driver. 'Your car is still in your garage,' the taxi driver said.

'Yes, it is still in the garage. Here is the key. Drive it home if you can. I know your home. You and your master come from the same place.'

'Yes, we come from the same place. But I want to buy your car,' he said. 'I want to make it a taxi.'

'Never mind about buying my car. Go to my garage early tomorrow morning, or this morning. It is half past one now. Drive the car to your place and leave it there. When there is trouble, drive it home. It is a new car. I bought it only six months ago. You hear. This is not the time to talk about a car. I am told there is going to be trouble. If you have a family, take them home tomorrow.'

'You are running away then,' the taxi driver said.

'Yes. I am running away.' He was ashamed to say it, a soldier, running away. He should have stayed in his house, and got shot at night in his bed. He shuddered to think of it.

There was a sound from afar. A train was arriving. The station master came and told him that he could go in that one. Okay took the station master's hand. He led him to a solitary place in the station. 'If you hear anything, send your wife and children home.'

'I have sent my wife and children home,' he said.

'That's wise.'

'Is anything wrong?'

'I don't know. I cannot tell you. All is not well. But since you have sent your wife and children home, you are all right.'

'I understand you. Where do you come from?' Okay told him. He gripped his hand firmly in friendship. 'I understand you,' he said again. 'I understand you very well. Our people,' he said, and shook his head.

The train stopped and Okay jumped in, in the guard's van. He was still in his military uniform. The guard had already been told about him.

In the train, Okay was uneasy. If he reached Enugu, what

112

was he going to tell his office there? Was the plan only for Kaduna alone? Wasn't it going to affect those at Enugu also? If he was in time, he could avert the disaster there. By doing what?, he asked himself. By exposing the plot. What plot? His driver did not tell him of any plot. He merely told him that there was going to be trouble. The nature of the trouble, he did not know. He did not ask. He was not in a position to ask. And his boss? He did not want to think of that. He told him. It was his duty to tell his boss, and he told him. But why was he believing what his driver said to him? Wasn't it possible that the driver might be wrong, that nothing was going to happen after all. No, the more he thought of it, the more he was convinced that his driver knew what he was talking about.

When Okay opened his eyes, it was already daybreak. He was not disturbed in his sleep by the movement of the train. He rubbed his eyes, and looked about him. The train was still in motion. The guard came round and offered him a cup of tea. It was a welcome offer. He took it with gratitude and thanked him heartily.

'Last night, or early this morning, we could not talk,' the guard began. 'I could see you were very tired and a bit far away. My name is Okoye. I am from Awgu.' He stretched his hand. Okay gripped it, but he did not immediately introduce himself. All Mr. Okoye knew was that Okay was an army officer. That was enough for him at the moment.

'You are going to Enugu?', Okay asked.

'Port Harcourt,' Mr. Okoye corrected. 'Port Harcourt and then retirement. I am due now at home. My daughters tell me I should return, as if I don't know I am overdue for it. But my fear is, what will I do at home? I have worked in the railways for the past twenty-six years. Occasionally, I went home, during my leave to see home people. But I have never belonged to home people. I don't understand their ways, and I don't think they understand mine.'

Okay wanted very badly to tell the old man to keep quiet, that he was busy with his own thoughts, that he was not in

113

the least interested in what he was saying, that what he was saying was not important to him nor to anybody for that matter. But the old man went on: 'I first went to Jos. That was my first place of appointment. I lived with my brother for one year, then I got a room of my own. I saved money and went home and married a wife. She was a lovely village girl. I married her in the church. And we had all our children there in Jos. Jos is a lovely place. In those days, at the end of each month, I would give my wife ten shillings for food. It was more than enough. She had a cassava and yam farm. She had a vegetable farm as well. She kept chickens. My colleagues told me ten shillings was too much, but I did not worry. I let her have it. She was such a lovely girl, and I did not want to appear stingy. I thought I was going to retire there, in Jos. I had built two houses. I would retire in one. But the trouble came. It couldn't be the people I knew so well, not the people whom I lived with all those years who were guilty of the murder, the arson and the rape. Not them, I kept on telling my wife. I said, it couldn't be these people. But they were the same people, my son, the same people. God, who turned their hearts against us, they were such good people, who did this?'

Mr. Okoye did not seem to be talking to anybody in particular, because it did not matter to him whether Okay was listening or not. He was talking out of the fullness of his heart. It was then that Okay was forced to listen to him in spite of the fact that he was weighed down by his own thoughts and problems. 'You must thank your God that you are now going home. What happened before would be a child's play compared to what would happen in the next day or two,' Okay said. As soon as he said it, he regretted saying it. He shouldn't have said it. He was a soldier. Their words carried weight these days. Okay was conscious of this, and was careful in what he did and said. He hated the thoughtlessness of some of his colleagues in asserting themselves anywhere they went. The army takeover meant something deeper for him than mere taking

114

over from where the politicians left off.

Mr. Okoye did not know the gravity of what Okay said, because he did not take it up. He did not say, 'My son, is it true what you are saying? Are my people going to have a bad experience, worse than what they had before? And what are we going to do about it, or you in the armed forces, going to do about it? We look on you.' Okay expected to hear this, but he did not. Mr. Okoye rather asked, 'Are you going on leave?' Okay said he was going on leave. The old man's face showed that he did not believe him. He knew it himself, but he said nothing. He felt he had already talked too much. He wasn't going to say any more.

'You have no luggage, and you are travelling in a goods train. Tell me, is anything wrong?' Okay was impressed to hear this. He liked the way the old man got about it. He had misjudged him.

'I don't know,' Okay heard himself saying. 'Honestly, I don't know, but I suspect something. That's why I am running away.'

'That's why you are running away,' Mr. Okoye said. He was afraid. 'Something is wrong then. Mere suspicion would not make you leave your post.'

'It could involve my life,' Okay said, a bit lightly.

'I am not a child. I know what I am saying. So they are going to start killing us again, as they did before?'

'That's what I suspect.'

Breakfast was brought this time. It was a big breakfast. Okay looked at his watch and saw that it was only nine o'clock. They must have been up early. There was every indication that Okay was included in the breakfast. He couldn't remember when last he had yam and stew for breakfast. He did not want to be discourteous, by saying that he was not going to have breakfast. So he took his plate, cut a slice into two, took one, put it in his plate, and spooned a piece of fish from the bowl into it, and began to eat. All the time, Mr. Okoye watched him.

'Is that all you are going to eat?' he asked.

'Yes, I am not hungry really, and besides, I don't have yam and stew for breakfast.'

'I thought as much. We have bread and butter. I thought this would be better. I knew you were hungry,' he ended.

Hungry, did he look hungry? That was serious. Perhaps he looked it. He had just tea yesterday morning. He didn't eat anything again until then. The old man was right. 'Don't worry about the bread and butter. This will do for me,' he said.

Okay watched Mr. Okoye as he devoured the yam and stew meant for both of them. Then he asked for beer. They brought two bottles for him. Okay drank his with relish. That was what he wanted more than food, beer. What could take the place of beer? Nothing. 'We shall have beer again, my son,' Mr. Okoye said. 'I can see you enjoy your beer like I do. Every day, for the past fifteen years, I have always washed down my breakfast with beer, cold beer. This is not cold, but beer is beer whether cold or hot.'

They had another bottle, and another, then another. Okay said he wasn't drinking any more. 'Only four beers? You are a young man. You should drink six at a sitting. When I was your age, I used to drink a dozen at a time. We enjoyed life in those days. There is so much to do these days, that young men don't enjoy life, don't know how to enjoy themselves. I tell my children that the greatest gift from God is the gift for capacity to enjoy oneself in any circumstance.'

They travelled on. What an interesting companion, old as Mr. Okoye was. Okay felt better. He wasn't running away. He was having a good trip. He could not remember when last he had such an interesting train journey. The last he could remember was when he was in school. It was such a wretched journey that he vowed never to travel by train in Nigeria any more.

It wasn't easy to push the thought of what was happening in Kaduna to the back of his mind, the guard notwithstanding. If anything was to happen, it had happened, or it was still happening. His boss, was he alive or dead? He would know when he got to Enugu. Mr Okoye had told him that they would reach Enugu the following day in the evening. He would know then. It wasn't long to wait.

Then Okay remembered his fiancee. That was the first time he remembered her since he took the file containing her letters, and left his house. She was in Lagos. He wasn't very happy with her when he went to Lagos. She did not behave nicely to him and he knew the cause. What was the point leaving her in Lagos? She had suggested that the best thing would be to get married in Lagos and then go to Kaduna with him. But Okay did not want to get married just then. There was no strong reason for it, he did not feel like it then. And his fiancee had interpreted it in the way that suited her. She accused him of lack of love and consideration. If there was a serious upheaval in Lagos, she would return. Perhaps she might not return. He did not like what he saw in Lagos. His fiancee was getting more and more involved in Lagos life, and it might be difficult, unless she was threatened with death to be uprooted from Surulere where she lived. It was his fault, not hers, and if anything should happen to her, he would have himself to blame.

At a station, the train stopped, and the guard went down, and bought some foodstuff, and more beer. Okay was not interested in the station. Nothing attracted, him not even the naked bodies of women returning from the market, with large baskets on their heads. Nudity had never attracted him. Those men who were attracted by the naked bodies of women, were neurotic. The vice he refused to indulge in, when he spent a fortnight in Paris, was paying money to see a strip tease.

It occurred to Okay that he hadn't mentioned anything about fare to Mr. Okoye. He was sleeping. When he woke up, he would ask him. He wasn't giving him a ride in the goods train for nothing. So when he woke up, he asked him how much he was going to pay. At first Okay thought Mr. Okoye did not hear, so he repeated the question.

'You children, when would you learn? So if I am in your

117

position, you would take money from me? Can't we do a good turn for our fellow countryman without thinking of money? Money indeed. If I do a good turn for my son, I should be paid for it, eh? Is that why you have not told me your name? You children think you are clever.'

Okay was full of apologies. It was not so. He had meant to tell him, but he forgot. He was very sorry, he must forgive him. His name was so and so. The name clicked at once. 'You are my friend's son. You don't mean it. Your father was with me for a short while in Kaduna in 1950. Then he was transferred back to Port Harcourt. We had just met, and were about to be good friends, when he was transferred. You were a little kid then. And where is he now?'

'He is dead.'

'No,' Mr. Okoye exclaimed.

'He died two years ago.'

'And your mother?'

'She is well. She is at home.'

'You are going home to her, aren't you?'

It was then that it occurred to Okay that the best thing he could do when he got to Enugu was go straight to his mother and sister.

'Yes I shall go home to see them first.'

'Remember me to your mother. Tell her Herbert Okoye asked about her. The world is so small. My good friend. He knew how to live. It was your father who taught me to live well. I learnt my expensive habits from him. And I don't regret it. I have never regretted it. I am glad you are going home. Go home, my son. When things are normal again, you shall return.'

The journey continued to be very smooth until they reached Enugu. Mr. Okoye had given Okay his shirt. It was not necessary to be in uniform. He had no time to study the faces of the people he saw on the platform. He was aware that there were many people at the train station. He hailed a taxi. 'Awka,' he said. He did not even hear what the taxi driver said. He went in, and banged the door.

118

There was light in the house. Okay paid the driver, and walked towards the house. It was his sister he first saw, and called her by her name. She shuddered, then ran to him. He held her close, feeling safe as he did so. 'Mama,' his sister shouted. 'Mama, Okay is back. Okay is alive, Okay is not dead.' Their mother sat on the floor where she had been sitting since they heard the news of the coup. Neighbours, friends and well-wishers had gone home, leaving the few close friends of Okay's mother.

Okay sat on the floor with his mother, his hand round her neck. 'God, I thank you,' was all she could say. She was overwhelmed. She was not given to open demonstration of affection.

'He is back, he is back, my only brother is back,' his sister shouted for everybody to hear. The people came out in large numbers to welcome their son who was fortunate to return.

A woman came forward, more alive than dead, as the people were going back to their houses. Okay saw her and went to her. He took her hand. 'Did you see him?' Okay shook his head. 'I didn't see him before I left. I saw him before I went to Lagos. He told me he was travelling abroad. If he left the day he told me he would leave, then he is safe.'

'Do you say so, my son?'

'I think so. He told me what I have just told you. Nothing will happen to him if he is abroad.'

The woman thanked him and went away. Okay went into the room. His mother and sister were there.

'My son, I am grateful to God.'

'So am I mother,' Okay said.

'What happened? How did you manage to escape?'

'I shall tell you.'

# My Soldier Brother

I remember my brother Adiewere very well. He was my eldest brother. I was not fond of him until Mother died. Everybody was crying. My sisters and my brothers were all crying. I cried because I saw them crying. It hadn't dawned on me that I was not going to see Mother again. I must have been seven years old then. My brother, Adiewere, carried me on his lap as I cried like the others. He was the only one who did not cry. Father made frightening noises. His was a deep voice. I was so frightened because that was the first time I heard him make such noises. I remember the procession as they led Mother's coffin to the graveyard. I remember that at night Father called all of us together and told us to be brave and stick together, that God would protect us, and that he would rather starve than see us in want. I watched Adiewere's face. There was no expression on it. His face frightened me. My brothers and sisters cried again, but he did not cry.

Adiewere and the others went back to school. I remained at home with my two sisters and three brothers. I had five brothers and five sisters, but I did not consider it a very large family. I remember telling Mother excitedly one day before she died that I wanted ten brothers and six sisters. I did not know how I came about those numbers but I remember the numbers very well. I remember that Mother laughed and said I did not know what I was talking about.

Soon Adiewere got his school certificate. He passed in grade one. We were very happy. Father was beside himself with joy. I knew why. It was because our elder brother bluntly refused to go on after he reached class four. My

120

father pleaded but he refused to go on. And he was not dull at all. There was a time he came fifth in his class. Father went to the 'Esquire' and bought Adiewere a suit, a tie and pair of shoes. I knew that he had been saving quietly for this for a long time. Otherwise, it would have been difficult for him to pay cash for them. In the evening, we killed a goat in celebration. We invited our uncles and our aunts. They were all very pleased.

Of all my aunts, I remember Aunt Monica at that celebration. She was very happy, and danced around while nobody was dancing. Then to the embarrassment of every-body, she called my eldest brother, and commanded him to come and stand before her. He stood before her. 'You must be ashamed of yourself now. Here is your younger brother. He has passed his exams with honours, and you, you refuse to read on. You stubborn child, who told you your father was as poor as not to be able to pay your fees? It is your funeral, not mine. Soon, your brother would go to the University, graduate and have a car, and you, you will be carrying his bag for him when he comes home on leave like Oputa carried your father's bag (Oputa was my uncle who lost the opportunity to go to school because he feared the teacher's whips). You think the pennies they are paying you mean anything, wait, time will tell you . . .'

'Monica, it is enough. Stop your nonsense here. Who asked you to say all this? Did you call Mike and talk to him seriously two years ago when he left school? Didn't I come to your house and complain to you? What did you say to me? If you had forgotten, let me remind you. You said I should leave him to do as he wished, that there were so many children who read up to class four and obtained good jobs, senior service jobs with cars. Wasn't it you who said it, two years ago? Why are you being unkind to him now? It was you, you who misled him, you, you and nobody else. And let me tell you . . .'

By this time, Father had got up, and my aunt was up too. I could hear only my aunt's loud voice. 'Odinibe, did you say

121

that I misled your son, that I misled your son. God, who is in the skies, please hear my voice this night. If I misled my brother's son, let me not see the break of day tomorrow. Send your thunder and kill me this minute, this very minute. 'Utousi', 'Nganaga' 'Akpu nwa ngworo' hear me this night. Kill me instantly if I misled my brother's son. Cut off my tongue, my . . .'

'Look, look, wait, swallow your saliva. You will die, Monica, your mouth will kill you one day. I was there that day. It was in your house. Odinibe came to your house to tell you. What he said just now was exactly what you said. So keep quiet if you don't want to die. We have come here to celebrate, not to quarrel,' my eldest uncle said. Then he turned to my eldest brother, who was busy eating his goat meat. He had a nonchalant expression on his face. 'Don't mind Monica, my son. God had written what everybody would be in His big book. The water God said you would drink, you would drink. Nobody would take it from you.'

'So I am the one going to take the water my brother's son is going to drink from him? Is that what you are saying, eh, the eldest of our father's children? All right, I am going.'

She untied her headtie, retied it, untied her wrappa, retied it and walked out of the sitting room. I could not help thinking that she did all these hoping that one of us would beg her not to go. None of us begged her. Everybody was angry. Adiewere particularly was angry. It showed on his face, and I saw that he clenched his fists, Adiewere was quiet, but very deep. He never argued with Father. But he did not do what he did not want to do. I admired him very much, but sometimes, I was afraid of him. There was something in him. Something impenetrable, even mysterious about him. I could not understand what he felt for Aunt Monica. We all did not like her and said so amongst ourselves. But Adiewere didn't easily tell us or other people his likes and dislikes. Many times, he took me to see Aunt Monica. Sometimes she gave us food to eat, some other times she told us she had no food, that we should go home and cook, because there was

122

plenty of food at home, and we were only lazy. Adiewere did not get annoyed as I thought he would. He merely smiled in his quiet way, and said, 'Aunt Monica, you know I like to see you always. I don't come here to eat. I come to see you and to hear you talk.' Then Aunt Monica would laugh and order soft drinks and biscuits for us, and would then proceed to demolish the reputation of all our uncles and our aunts, except of course our Father's. We neither remembered nor verified what she said to us, for we knew that none of what she said about any of our relations was true.

Adiewere went back to school after the Christmas holiday. It was the happiest Christmas holiday that we had since the death of Mother. There was so much to eat and plenty of soft drinks. And besides, Adiewere took me to see his school friends and to the cinema. It was the only time he took me out when he was home. I believed that he was beginning to like me. He was already my hero.

I was surprised that he should go back to school. I thought he was going to get a job in the big town so that I could live with him. It was my ambition to live with him, serve him, run errands for him. I had thought that school certificate was the end of the road in his school career. But he told me that he was going back to school so that he would go to the University. His ambition was to read law. I did not like the idea of his reading law. I did not think he would be able to do well as a lawyer. Lawyers were garrulous and Adiewere was not. In fact he was too quiet and withdrawn. To my childish thinking, lawyers were meant to be open, forward, even aggressive. Adiewere did not possess any of these qualities. But then, he was my hero. He knew what he wanted to do in life, and who was I to criticise him.

Soon again Adiewere passed his higher school certificate examination, again with honours. We jubilated in our home. I was so happy, so very happy. My eldest brother was home on leave. Instead of killing a goat as we did when Adiewere passed his school certificate, my father took all of us to a studio, and we took a family photograph. In the evening, my

123

eldest brother took Adiewere and our two eldest sisters out to drink. I pleaded with him to take me, but he refused. He said I was too young to go out and drink. I said I would drink only soft drinks. They all laughed. I did not understand why they laughed. Then one of my sisters told me that it did not matter whether I drank water there. The point was that I was not of age.

'When will I be of age?' I asked stubbornly.

'When you are in a University,' she said without thinking.

'But you are not in a University. None of you is in fact in a University,' I said. Then Adiewere rubbed my head.

'Don't mind sister,' he said. 'When you are big, like brother,' he said pointing at our eldest brother, 'I shall take you out to drink.' That made sense to me. I did not understand my sister. But who understood sisters, who took them seriously anyway? They were all women, weak creatures. Men were strong, especially men like Adiewere.

I watched Father that day Adiewere received his result. He was happy no doubt, but he was restless. Perhaps happiness made some people restless. Perhaps he was thinking of the University fees he was going to pay when Adiewere went to a University. He remained in that mood for days, until one day Adiewere received a telegram. I don't remember where it came from. Adiewere jumped up, rushed to my father and handed the telegram to him. I was behind him, including my brothers and sisters who were at home. Father read the telegram. I watched his face. He did not jump like us. It was not that he was old. Father was not old. He had eleven children. He was young. He was the only child of his mother in a polygamous family. So his mother was anxious that he should marry early. He told us he married at the age of eighteen, but I believe that he must have married at the age of sixteen. Bringing us up was not a problem to Mother. Grandmother did all the rearing until she died. It was only when she died that my mother experienced the hardship, and the joy and agony of child rearing. For before Grandmother died, Mother turned us over to her when we were about nine months old. We remained with her until we reached school age.

Father was not outwardly excited like us, as he read the telegram aloud. Adiewere had won a scholarship to the University of Lagos. He would read English there. I could penetrate Father's heart and saw the happiness written with bold ink there. He sat where he sat when we all rushed in. His hands shook a little. That was the only outward excitement I saw in him that afternoon since the day he challenged Aunt Monica.

Aunt Monica was the first to come to our house. She was always the first to hear good and bad news, and come to congratulate or sympathise with us. I ran to the neighbours and told them of my brother's fortune. They poured in to congratulate us. I remember one old man particularly who said that Adiewere's fortune was like one waking up one morning, and seeing his empty barn full of yams. I frowned. It was not like that at all. The impression was that my brother was idle. He was not. I saw him nearly every night, when others went to bed, reading with the hurricane lamp in his room. I spent many nights with him, and knew that he was a great swot. Who gave the impression that he was not?

What made the news so exciting was the fact that Adiewere did not mention to anybody that he had applied for a scholarship. So the scholarship came as a pleasant surprise to everybody except of course Adiewere himself. I imagined his state of mind if he had been disappointed. As proud as he was, he would have suffered his failure quietly and with fortitude.

At night, I went to his room. I opened his big books and closed them. I fidgeted with this and that.

'So you finished reading all these books?' I asked him. He nodded, and went on with what he was doing.

'So when I am as big as you are, I am going to read all these books before I pass my exams.'

He stopped reading and looked at me in admiration. I was so pleased.

'What class are you now?' I told him. 'What subject do you like best?'

'Arithmetic,' I said without waiting for him to complete his sentence.

'You'll do engineering then,' he said.

'Engineering?' I asked.

'Yes. Those who know arithmetic do engineering.'

'Will I be able to make a car if I do engineering?' I asked, so thrilled. He laughed, but did not answer. I did not want to press him. Then I asked him, 'But you said you were going to be a lawyer. Why are you going to read English now?'

'A friend advised me to apply for English, that if I applied for English, I would win a scholarship. He was right. When I get to the University of Lagos, I would change to law, if they would let me.'

'And if they don't let you?'

'Well . . .' He did not say more. I knew that his words were not in vain.

In September 1966, Father saw Adiewere off at Onitsha. Aunt Monica was waiting for him when he returned. Father frowned when he saw her. But Aunt Monica was insensitive. She neither looked at your face nor listened to what you said to her when she thought she had displeased you. Father was too tired. He just wanted to drop in a chair, have a beer and then have his meal before he went to bed. 'Monica, don't you think you should come tomorrow? I am so tired,' Father said. He had been entangled in her web.

'Odinibe,' she shouted, 'have you greeted me? I am older than you are, you know.' Father laughed.

'Who are you older than, Monica?' he asked still laughing in a tired way.

'I was born in the evening, and you were born the following day, in the morning.' Father laughed. Aunt Monica never said the correct thing. Father had told me that both of them were born on the same day. He was born in the morning, and she in the evening.

Aunt Monica got up. 'I am going. I have come to tell you

126

that you are a fool to send your son to Lagos while those in Lagos are returning home. You went to school. Don't you read the newspapers? Go and bring our son back. You did not go to a University. He can get a good job here. I can take him to a man who would give him a job, right away.'

'You are right, I am wrong. Go to your home and leave me in peace Monica. Leave me in peace.'

'I am going to my home. Thank God I have a home. But if anything happens to Adiewere, you are responsible. They are killing our people this minute in Lagos. If you go to Lagos now, you would see corpses of our people in the streets of Lagos.'

My blood ran cold. I had heard of the killings in the North, but not in Lagos. Surely horrible things happened in Lagos, but I did not think it was as bad as Aunt Monica said. She was such a woman. She magnified stories. I remember when I was a little boy, I cut my finger with a razor blade. Unfortunately for me, Aunt Monica was at our house. Instead of doing something about it, she ran to the church and told my mother who was at a meeting that I had cut off my finger.

That night, I shivered in my bed. If anything should happen to my brother, then I too would die. Every day, we heard horrible reports of Lagos. We did not know what to make of these reports. And Adiewere had not written. Had he been killed? It was true that he was not a good letter writer. Father complained of this several times when Adiewere was in school, but he did not seem to do anything about it. He just did not write letters. Often again, I had heard him and his girl friends quarrelling in his room because he did not reply to their letters.

At last, one day, Adiewere's letter arrived. Father was pleased. He showed it to us. He told him that Lagos was all right, that there was no cause for alarm, that he was getting on well with his course, and that we should not heed what people and the newspapers said.

But every day, hundreds of our people returned from

Lagos. Father began to worry again. They told us stories which father did not know whether to believe or not. They said there were shootings in Lagos. Our people were being killed every day. They said women dug graves for the bodies of our men. Oh, it was too much. Father wrote and begged Adiewere to come home. He knew fully well that if he came home, that would mean the end of his scholarship. But life was more important than a scholarship. He could get a job when he came home. Perhaps, he could even be admitted into the University which was near us.

Adiwere did not reply to my father's letters. Then I wrote him. I told him I was on my knees begging him to come home, that we were all afraid, that he should please pity Father who would die if anything happened to him. I did not receive a reply.

Then one day a taxi stopped, and Adiewere emerged. Father grabbed him, grabbed him as if he belonged to him alone and not to all of us. We helped him bring out his suitcase and a box containing his books. All our relatives and friends came to welcome him. They asked him about Lagos and he told them that Lagos was all right. There was no trouble. Why then did he return? He said it was pressure from home.

It was when we were together that he told us why he returned. Lagos was safe for him until there was a rumour that a lecturer in Nsukka who was from the West was murdered by his students while he was lecturing. He said that immediately he heard the rumour, he and a few of his friends packed their belongings in thirty minutes and left. It was a dangerous rumour. Adiewere's immediate plan was to go to Nsukka to see if he would be enrolled. When he got there, he was surprised to see that everything was normal there.

Adiewere enrolled and then returned to take his suitcase and his books. I saw that he was not happy. He preferred the University of Lagos. He had told his friends when he was at school that he did not want to go to that University. They laughed at him. They told him they did not mind which

128

University they went provided they went to a University. They laughed at him for ever thinking that the University of Lagos, where good staff resigned en masse was better than the one at home.

I remember that there was much trouble in that University. Father and his friends talked so much about it that I was sick to hear of it. Father had come home from work one day to announce that our people had all resigned from the University. He was sad. It was a surprise to me therefore that Adiewere preferred that University to our own. But he knew best.

Adiewere made no friends at the University. There were many of his school boys who were there with him, but he did not have anything to do with them. He did go to political meetings, but he said nothing when he went there. I did not know whether he was unhappy for when he came home on holiday, he was more than quiet and withdrawn. He did not go out. His girl friends no longer came to see him. My sisters pleaded with him to take them out, but he refused. All he did during the holiday was sleep, read, eat occasionally and of course listen to music. I did not like the kind of records he played. They sang like birds in the forest, and I could not dance to them. My eldest sister had plenty of records that I liked. I did not bother myself to find out who bought these records or where she got money to buy all the records. We liked the records for they were the latest ones, and we enjoyed them.

It wasn't long after Adiewere had come home on long vacation, that our Military Governor declared the zero hour. Father was restless, everybody was restless. War at last. It was welcome news. The people were feverish with excitement. I heard sayings like this: 'Let them come by sea, land or air, we are ready for them.' I was excited myself, because the adults were excited. What did I know about war? Father did tell us about the last war in which a brother of his lost his life. He also said that things were scarce, and that many people died because they could not have salt. It was all so intriguing to me.

Adiewere was not excited. He was very calm but I watched him. I asked him about the war. I asked him what would happen if Biafra lost the war. He said that the northerners would rule us forever. That frightened me. Northerners suddenly became devils. I remember a lovely Fulani girl who sold kola nuts in the market. Each time Mother (that was when she was alive) sent me to the market to buy kola and other things, I made sure that I bought from her. If she were hawking it in the market, I would wait for her to return, or went all over the market in search of her. She did not only give me a shilling worth of kola for six pence, but she also gave me groundnuts. I liked the way she spoke our language, and the smile on her face when she saw me. My face also lit up each time I saw her. I did not know where she lived or who her mother was, and she did not know where I lived or who my mother was.

I liked her so much. Even when I had nothing to buy from the market, I went there just to see her smile at me and talk to me and give me groundnuts and sometimes, even sweets.

Adiewere left home one day with his suitcase. He had told Father that he was going to stay a few days with Aunt Monica. He did not reach Aunt Monica's house. The next that we heard was that he had joined the army. Father said nothing. We all watched him. His face was exactly the face he wore when Mother died. My sisters began to cry. My brothers and I did not cry. We behaved like our father. I wondered why women cried so easily. I was a man and I was not going to let my sisters see my tears. Suddenly, Father began to scold my sisters.

'Why are you crying, you fools? Every day you see hundreds of soldiers marching past and you clap for them, sing their songs and admire them. Now your brother has joined the army to save Biafra, and you are making so much noise. Let me hear any of you crying again, and I will break her neck.'

Father frightened me. The quiet that reigned after the

scolding frightened me. It was a long tie since I saw him in that mood. Since Mother died, he had become quieter and quieter every day. Somehow I could not help to notice that the outward calm was forced. It was put on so as to hide the inward turbulence. He might not have known, but I saw the fear in him as he scolded my sisters. Fear could make us do all sorts of things, both cowardly and brave.

I could not understand why Adiewere behaved in the way he did. He could have discussed it with Father. I knew Father. I knew he would have told him all the implications, that joining the army meant saving his country. It also meant death. I knew Father could not have stood in his way.

When Aunt Monica heard, she came. She came very early before six o'clock. When there was trouble or illness, she came very early in the morning to make more trouble. I heard her in the sitting room as she was scolding Father for letting Adiewere join the army. She called him all sorts of names. Father said nothing. Sometimes, sisters were such troublesome people. She ended by saying that Father should go to Enugu and see the Military Governor about Adiewere. She was sure that if he saw him, he would hand Adiewere over to him. Father said not a word.

Two months after, Adiewere came home. It was so dramatic. He hadn't written to anyone. And all of us were afraid to mention him for fear we would upset Father. But we, I particularly, remembered him every moment of the day. He was looking like his old self. He was thin a little. I loved him in his uniform. He was so smart. He was a first lieutenant. He laughed all the time and talked and joked.

He was in such a happy mood. I hadn't seen him in such a happy mood before. Father held him, held him as if he was afraid to let him go. We fired questions at him about the war, how our army was doing in all sectors of the war, as if he fought in all the sectors. He did not say much. 'We are doing very well,' was all he said. He told us so many jokes which I have forgotten because I was not interested in the jokes. I was interested in Adiewere as a soldier.

131

I was so proud of him. I told all my friends about him and they came to see him to touch his uniform and his gun. He took us out on a ride many times, and bought us groundnuts. There were no biscuits and sweets anywhere. I showed him our trenches which we dug behind our house. He laughed and laughed. 'These are no trenches,' he said. 'Before I go, I am going to dig trenches for you.' So I told everybody that my soldier brother was going to dig trenches for us.

Adiewere had no time to dig the trenches. He was recalled. He had five days more to stay, but his unit recalled him. Father held his hand in his for a long time. 'Go well my son. God will save and protect you.' It wasn't a week after that we received Adiewere's letter saying that he was a full lieutenant.

When Adiewere left, I joined the militia. It was not dramatic. I went to Father and told him. He said it was all right, if I was sure in my mind that the decision was mine. I told him that the decision was mine, and that I was going to discharge my duties, after my training, with courage like Adiewere.

At first I went from home. But later, as the training progressed, I went to live in the camp. I liked the camp food. I did not bother at all what I ate. I wondered how Adiewere was faring in the army. He was so particular about his food. There were so many foods he could not eat. And he preferred to go hungry rather than eat those foods.

I enjoyed the training, to the surprise of Father and my brothers and sisters. I did not look strong. I was thin and all bones. I taught my brothers and sisters how to take cover. They tended to hide when they were taking cover.

After about five weeks, we were told that we would go somewhere. We all thought that it was Enugu. Enugu front had been bad of recent. We were not told exactly, but we knew. Then, a few days after, we were told we were not going anymore. I was disappointed. We went on with our training, and the war continued.

Father came home one afternoon in tears. Yes, in tears. His eyes were red. He aged that moment. Adiewere had been

132

mortally wounded. There was little hope. Father never mixed words. Why give us hope when there was no hope? The girls again wept as they wept when Mother died. Father had wiped his tears. He went to the hospital with our eldest sister, and brother. They were just in time. Adiewere held Father's hand, and died.

He had died before I came in. Yes, I followed them. I would not be left behind. The young doctor who gave Adiewere blood stood there with Father and my brothers and sisters. 'I don't think he is dead,' I said to the doctor. 'He does not look dead,' I said again. 'Give him an injection to revive him. Do something, can't you, can't you, can't you . . .'

The young doctor held me. There were tears in his eyes. 'There is nothing I can do. He is dead.'

By this time, my sisters were wailing and then Aunt Monica ran in. I wondered how she knew. She fell on the corpse that was Adiewere, and gave out a frightful cry. Everybody in the ward, who could walk, that is, came. She called my father all sorts of names as she wept, blamed him for Adiewere's death,and recounted the good things she did for Adiewere, and regretted that he did not live to repay her.

Somehow, we all went home. There our uncles and aunts and other relations came. Since Adiewere was an officer, he was going to have a full military burial. The army was responsible then for the burial. We just waited for them, and we would go and bury him.

The next day, sympathizers poured in. Aunt Monica behaved as if she was the chief mourner. She sat talking nonsense all the time. I felt like asking her out of the house, but then I could not do it. I was a little boy. I looked after my younger brothers and sisters. They were hungry. Aunt Monica who was so near us did not even think of taking them to give them food in her house. What our people said about her that she starved her husband to death was probably true.

I was sitting at a corner, when one of Father's friends came. He gripped Father's hand, and said, 'Adiewere died

133

an honourable death. He died that you and I and all of us here might live. You should be proud of your son.' He pressed an envelope in Father's hand and left. He did not sit down and drink like the others. He was Father's closest friend, though he did not come often to our house. Father told us they were in school together.

Immediately he turned his back, Aunt Monica burst out: 'I am tired of people coming here and talking rubbish. What death is honourable? Death is death. A good and an intelligent boy died, and old men who should die say he died honourably. The sooner they stop talking of honourable death, the better.' Nobody answered her. Jolly good. Why shouldn't Aunt Monica keep quiet and behave like other women?

One of our aunts who lived about six miles away took us in a taxi to her house and fed us well. I was grieved, but I was hungry. Though the food did not taste good in my mouth, I forced myself to eat. My little brothers and sisters ate.

The next day, the burying squad brought Adiewere in a beautiful coffin, that is if a coffin could be decribed as beautiful. There were also some members of his battalion who fought in the battle in which he received his wound. They were all armed.

The coffin was placed in the sitting room before it was carried to the church. Everybody wept again. Father did not weep. The procession was long and impressive. The service was brief, the sermon brief, and what's more to the point. Adiewere died that we might live.

After the burial, we returned home. Father was exhausted. My brothers and sisters were exhausted. The youngest cried all the time. He was barely eight years old. Did he understand? Did he know that we would never see our soldier brother again?

A week later, I was called. We were going to the front. What front I did not know. I was thrilled. I was going to avenge Adiewere's death. I did not mind dying. Father said nothing when I told him. My brothers and sisters wept afresh. It was a Friday that we all entered the train that took us to Enugu. I was going to get ten heads of the enemy before they got me.